Brutal

WOL-VRIEY

Burning Bulb
PUBLISHING

Other Books By Wol-vriey:

The Bizarro Story of I
Meat Suitcase
Chainsaw Cop Corpse
Vegan Zombie Apocalypse
Boston Posh (Bud Malone #1)
Vegan Vampire Vaginas
Vagina Mundi
Melanie Nemesis Catchpole
Bizarro 101: A Basic Primer
Boston Corpse (Bud Malone #2)
Dr. Orgasm
Boston Lust (Bud Malone #3)
Pussy Transmission
Hell Dancer
Girls Are Not Smiling
Brainchew
Brainchew 2: Out of Their Heads
Blue Nightmares
Daria (An Erotic Nightmare)
Wet Bones
Mr. Ugly

Novellas and Short Stories By Wol-vriey

Big Trouble in Little Ass
Forever Ago Sunshine

Brutal

WOL-VRIEY

Burning Bulb
PUBLISHING

Brutal
By **Wol-vriey**

Burning Bulb Publishing
P.O. Box 4721
Bridgeport, WV 26330-4721
United States of America
www.BurningBulbPublishing.com

Cover artwork by Paradise Studio/Alex Malikov and used under license from Shutterstock.

Author Photo: Lolade Akinsowon © 2014.

First Edition.

Paperback Edition ISBN: 978-1-948278-10-2

Printed in the United States of America

PROLOGUE: TWENTY YEARS AGO

Smoke. Fire. Intense heat. Screaming.

She was in the backseat, sitting beside her brother Jimmy. In the car's front seats, both of her parents were unconscious from the crash.

They were somewhere in the west Massachusetts countryside, on a pleasant if mostly deserted road. It was a sunny weekend afternoon. They'd been driving over to Plainfield see her Uncle Charlie and Aunt Margaret and her cousins. She and Jimmy had been arguing over something. Up front, her parents had been laughing about something on the radio.

Then her mother had yelled: "Look out!"

She and Jimmy had both looked up. They'd yelled too.

Their car had just turned a bend, when seeming out of nowhere an oncoming blue pickup truck had lost control and swerved across into their lane.

For a moment the huge out-of-control vehicle had filled the windscreen, then they'd smashed into its side. The front airbags had inflated then deflated; and now her father and mother were both unconscious, and the car was burning.

She and Jimmy were both screaming. She was eight years old, he was six, and the child safety locks were on—they couldn't get the doors open. Scared as they were, it was taking them forever to even get their seatbelt straps off.

"MOM! DAD! WAKE UP! WAKE UP!" This was Jimmy yelling and leaning forward to shake their father, who sat there limp in the driver's seat, a trickle of blood streaming from his nose. All Jimmy's shaking accomplished was to jerk their father's head about on his shoulders.

The little girl also leaned forward and began shaking their mother. (They'd each sat behind the parent of the same gender.) Beside her mother's right arm the car door had buckled inward from the pressure of the crash.

"MOM! THE CAR'S ON FIRE!"

To her relief, their mother grunted. It was a weak noise, but one that gave the young girl hope.

But meanwhile, the fire poured towards them like flooding water. It covered the hood of the car, engulfing it like a red-hot mouth. The world ahead of she and Jimmy was a wall of spreading flame. A wall that, inch by inch, moved forward towards them. Both she and her brother could feel the heat, burning towards them as if it was desperate to eat them.

She was still shaking her mother. Mother began screaming. The young girl wasn't sure if her mother had opened her eyes, seen the danger and screamed, or if she'd merely reacted to the pain of being burnt.

"PAUL! WAKE UP, BABY! THE CAR'S ON FIRE! Then Mother was leaning over between the seats and frantically trying to unlock the rear doors.

The doors didn't unlock. The rear ones because the crash had busted the child safety locks, the front one on Mother's side because the door frame was buckled inward, its top glassless half now forming warped metal bars that prevented exit through it. The door on Father's side might have been okay, but the dashboard had also buckled inward, meaning that exit was unreachable.

"Shit!" Mother screamed. "I can't get the doors open!" Both of the rear windows were rolled up, because Jimmy had a tendency to stick his hands outside the car while it was in motion. Now they wouldn't wind down because the dashboard was shattered.

A torrent of frantic noises spilling from her mouth, Mother leaned out through the window of her own buckled door and tried to force its lock from the outside. However, all she succeeded in doing was tearing her smart yellow dress and her arm, and burning herself on the hot metal and melting plastic.

Mother was looking around desperately. She began battering the pop-up sunroof. She knocked the sunroof out of the top of the car.

She grabbed Jimmy's arm. "Go, Jimmy! Go go go! Outside!"

But, the fire was outside and Jimmy was reluctant to go anywhere. The young girl grabbed him and forced him forward into her mother's reaching arms. Up Jimmy went, outwards toward safety.

But then, suddenly, the fire was everywhere, almost as if someone had emptied a bowl of red hot sparks over the car. Like a transfusion of fresh blood, the fire poured in through the top of the vehicle. Suddenly Jimmy, who'd been climbing to safety, was on fire and burning like a torch, and Mother was on fire too.

Jimmy fell back into the car. On instinct he scrambled back to his original place in the backseat and began trying to put himself out.

Mother grabbed Father, but he was already burning before she'd touched him—the hungry flames had flooded in through the open window on his side.

Father didn't wake up even then; he burnt quietly like a roast and melted up and became part of his seat and the dashboard. But Mother and Jimmy more than made up for the noise Father didn't make. Both were screaming blue murder; and Mother's red hair and the fire seemed one and the same thing, and her green eyes were wide with fright and agony. Her yellow dress was burning on her now and it also seemed a natural part of the flames.

The young girl was the only one not yet burning. Actually, she might have been on fire too, but she wasn't sure. She did feel a horrible pain in her right leg, but at that moment, her attention was distracted, so she didn't look at it.

Instead, she stared outside, through the window next to her. By now, the flames had completely engulfed the car and her fleeting glimpse of the surrounding pleasant countryside seemed more of a mirage than a reality. But she'd noticed something out there. Something that was taking her mind off the commotion and the heat and the pain she should be feeling.

She'd seen something nice. Something pretty and reassuring.

Then the flames blocked off her brief glimpse of the countryside and she was once again shut off inside the car, left with her mother's screams for help and Jimmy's burning hands on her back, and a smell like roast pork, and the pain of the hot metal seemingly melting her shoes into her feet, as the world around her became an inferno cooking everything.

But then the flames around the car parted again and she saw the 'something' again. And she smiled with delight when she saw it.

It was a rabbit. A large white fluffy rabbit, and it was coming towards the car to rescue her. It wasn't hopping, however. No, this particular rabbit seemed to be flying through the air.

"HELP US!" Mother screamed. "FOR GOD'S SAKE, SOMEBODY HELP US!"

But there was no one else driving the deserted road. No one to hear and help them. No one but the rabbit, which Mother apparently hadn't noticed yet.

The little girl began hoping that the nice fluffy white bunny would make it safely to the burning car. She hoped it would be able to help them.

Because now, she was on fire too.

It had taken a while, but the flames had seemingly gotten around to remembering her now, and seemed intent on cooking her too.

And the burning hurt like hell.

She began screaming. Louder even than both Mother and Jimmy combined.

PART 1: EVILS OF THIS PRESENT AGE

CHAPTER 1

Jane

As an adult, Jane Winters was the spitting image of her long-dead mother. She too was an attractive redhead with striking green eyes. She was neither fat nor thin, just very nicely proportioned, and was very well liked by everyone at the Worcester Cashstretch department store where she worked.

The primary visible difference between the woman of past memory and the one in present tense was their mouths; or rather in the settings of their lips: while Ellen Winters had laughed joyfully and readily, her single surviving offspring was on the whole, a lot more serious.

Jane Winters could and did smile often, but if one looked closely enough, one could see that the mirth didn't reach her eyes; or, on those occasions on which it did, it didn't linger long there, almost as if her mind had left her face to handle her social engagements and was itself busy elsewhere.

But by and large, everyone liked Jane. If she wasn't exactly the life of the party, the party seemed incomplete without her.

And Jane liked people too. Maybe a whole lot more than she should have.

CHAPTER 2

More Jane...

Jane's main souvenir of the fiery childhood accident in which her family had died was that she had no fingerprints. The tips of her fingers were as smooth as the skin on her cheeks, entirely lacking any ridges whatsoever.

Jane herself didn't understand how this was possible. The doctors said it must have happened while she was gripping the car door before being rescued; the flames had burnt all the palm-side finger skin away.

This explanation made some sense to Jane, but there were holes in its logic, the most obvious of these holes being that so far, no one had been able to give her a reason why the same raging inferno that had smoothened out the palm-sides of her fingers had had no effect whatsoever on the reverse side. Her fingernails were perfect; not one of them was damaged in any way. And when she thought back now, it had been that way ever since the bandages came off after the accident.

In Jane Winters' modern life, the main result of that past fire seemed to be an inability for the US government to keep proper track of her. Which nowadays did come in extremely useful.

CHAPTER 3

Jane

Jane noticed the young man the moment he walked in through the department store entrance.

It was a deceptively warm Wednesday in early June. Early evening at the time and Jane was just finishing up her shift. Thirty minutes more and she'd be out the door. She was expecting her boyfriend Scott to come over that night and planned on cooking a special dinner for both of them.

At the time the young man walked into Cashstretch, Jane was attending to a Goth teenager who'd bought a lot of cat food.

Smiling, Jane handed the girl her change and her receipt. The girl moved off. The next person in the queue stepped forward. This was a gaunt old man pushing a piled shopping cart; mostly microwaveable packs and breakfast cereals.

While helping the old man unload the topmost of his purchases onto the counter, Jane watched the young man who'd just entered. She watched him push an empty shopping cart towards the farther aisles, over where the organic and health foods were stocked.

Her eyes expertly appraised his form and his motion. He was tall and very muscular. In fact, he was dressed to show off his excellent physique, in a gray muscle shirt, tight black shorts, and white sneakers. All of him was displayed exactly how she liked it to be. It made 'choosing' easy.

He's really perfect, she thought.

Still unloading the old man's cart, she ran her eyes down the young man's body, then back up it again, searching for that exquisitely correct part of him that she just had to have. Then down once more. Quickly. Her Mr. Perfect had paused right before stepping into an aisle, and was now staring out through the storefront glass at the parking lot. Maybe he was looking for his car, a single amongst the many out there. Whatever the cause for his pause, it presented Jane with a wonderful opportunity to really look him over: once he stepped into the aisles, she'd not see him again until he came over to the checkout counters; and here, the counter would obscure her view of his lower body.

She admired his face (he was blonde, with a short fuzzy mustache and beard), his biceps, pecs, abs, and the firm shape of his groin. But her attention really stuck on his calf muscles. Before, when he'd been walking towards the aisles, she'd only gotten an impression of their actual size and shape. But now that he was turned towards the entrance, she got a proper look at the backs of his legs.

Yes, his thighs stood out in sculpted definition. But his calf muscles—just looking at those, she felt herself getting wet between the legs. The man's calves were massive and godlike.

I've never seen any so perfect, she thought coldly. *I must have him! He's mine!*

A raspy voice snapped her back into the moment.

"Miss Jane, I'm waitin'."

She turned back to the old customer at her station. "Oh, I'm sorry, sir. I got distracted for a minute." He'd gotten her name off the tag on her blue uniform blouse.

She flung a last glance over at the young man to ensure he wasn't about leaving without buying anything, then began scanning and bagging the old man's purchases.

She'd been partly wrong about what the old man was buying: it wasn't just microwaveable food. Just as the Goth girl she'd served before him had seemingly had a fascination with cats, this old guy seemed to have a lot of *dogs*. She scanned six different brands of dog food and eight packs of dog treats. Besides those, there were just seven microwave food packs, toiletries, and lots of tissue paper and wipes.

"Your total is eighty dollars, sixty cents, sir."

She watched him closely as he handed her his credit card. He wasn't going to be eating the dog food along with his pets, was he? But no, he didn't seem poverty-stricken at all. She guessed he was just a lonely old man who needed lots of canine friends to keep him company.

Jane ran the card through the cash register. His name was Joe Steckler. She handed back the card. While attending to the old man, she'd been studying his face intently, but carefully, so he didn't realize that she was doing so.

No, she told herself firmly, *he's too old. Much too old. Under those layers of thermal underwear, he's nothing but mottled sinew; skin like old leather, gristle and liver spots and fatless bones.* For a moment, Jane saw the old man clearly in her mind—stripped bare and laid out naked on a morgue slab. The image revolted her. An intense nausea rose up through her body and she struggled not to puke.

She hid her disgust with a smile, of course. Her reaction was merely the result of her personal take on things. Mr. Steckler here wasn't anything other than a lonely old man. She, however . . .

Mr. Steckler shambled off. Next in line was a teenager with a skateboard. Long brown hair, frayed and ripped jeans, sneakers, backpack, and a baseball cap turned back to front.

The boy was buying two music CDs and a *Call of Duty: Black Ops* video game. She took the items from him. The top CD was *Bitch Perfect*, Slain Jane's new album, with its pseudo-risqué cover art of Jane Orgasm butt-naked, but with her skin silvered up like she was an alien of some kind. Her nipples and pubic hair had been pixelated out of existence.

Jane grimaced. There was such a thing as taking liberty too far. A 'Jane' herself, and a fan of the band for that exact reason (though she never admitted as much to anyone), she felt scandalized by the extent to which Jane-O was prepared to stoop to sell CDs. (This wasn't their all-time low though—no, the inner sleeve for the *Antidote For God* album had shown an orgy featuring all the members of the band and their significant others, and with nothing being left to the imagination.)

Jane scowled at the CD cover again. Yes, for certain, Miss Orgasm was shapely, but her breasts looked like they'd just been reconstructed after a double mastectomy.

She scanned the kid's purchases, gave him his change, and he left, dropping his skateboard to the ground, and riding it towards the front entrance. Skateboarding definitely wasn't allowed inside Cashstretch but, since when did teens ever listen to anyone?

She watched him go. The sliding doors were automatic and if that boy didn't slow down already . . . Her mind unconsciously calculated his trajectory and the seconds to him hitting the glass head on. She could already see him with a long bloody shard sticking through his neck like he'd been skewered.

Not a bad image actually.

But, false mental alarm. The teen slowed, the doors opened, and he left alive.

Jane returned her attention into the supermarket. The skateboarding teen had been the last in her checkout queue. For the moment she had no one else to serve.

Jane was at the second checkout counter from the front doors. Of the eight checkout stations, two were empty. The flow of customers was low. Danielle, the woman on her left and closest to the entrance, seemed to be out on her feet. Jane thought Danielle was pregnant again but wasn't telling anyone the happy news yet. Her face had that healthy glow to it characteristic of women who'd enjoyed the 'joys of motherhood' a little bit too successfully in the near past.

Tony, who was stationed immediately to her right, had left to "use the staff restroom," five minutes ago. Jane smirked. Tall and skinny Tony Marler was certain to be back soon with his eyes unnaturally bright and his face all flushed. Jane wasn't deceived in the least. For certain, the guy was abusing some kind of narcotic, most likely cocaine. He couldn't be on pot. She'd have smelt that on him. Besides, Tony tended to act manic, never mellow.

Jane shrugged. It was merely a matter of time before their supervisor Mr. Ackerman found out and gave Tony the boot. None of her business, except that Tony was a friend of hers, pleasant to work alongside, and she'd hate to see him leave.

Where is he? Her eyes travelled down the row of cashiers, searching the farther reaches of the store for the young man with the perfect legs.

On the other side of Tony's vacant post, Melanie, Andy, Fatima, Jake and Mario were busily scanning barcodes and bagging purchases, swiping credit cards, and handing out change to a motley array of people.

Andy was having an argument with a fat woman who was insisting that her Walmart credit card should be usable in Cashstretch.

"No, ma'am," Andy was explaining, "you need a Cashstretch card for that. You can easily apply for one online. It'll be ready in a week."

Jane still had no one to serve. A man on her right seemed headed for her, but then detoured to Andy's counter instead when the fat woman he'd been arguing with left in a huff, pulling her young daughter after her.

The departing woman sniffed at the line of cashiers. "Come on, Annie, let's go. Make your bottom dollar go further, my ass!"

"Mommy, I want ice cream!" the girl (who seemed about five) howled as she was dragged away. "I want some ice cream!" She refused to move and dug her little feet in.

"Not in here, you don't!" her mother retorted, stooping to pick the young protester up and carry her off.

The pair passed Jane, the mother as red-faced as if she'd shortly defecate on herself.

Jane's station was still empty. As if she was giving off psychic vibrations that prevented people noticing she was available to serve them. This had happened before when she was on the hunt—people seemingly avoiding her until she'd made contact with her prey. Quickly now, before someone arrived and distracted her, she looked around for the young man with the perfect calves.

Where is he? I must have him! Again, she felt the familiar fire burn through her. From a secret source in her belly, the heat of desire rose like a balloon into her mind, and sank like lead down through her groin to her feet. It was a pleasant if overwhelming feeling. Thankfully, it didn't hurt like that other fire had: that fire of long ago which had robbed her of her family. What she felt now was close to full-blown sexual arousal.

However, from long practice, Jane was expert now at coping with her internal fire. She restrained herself from gasping or moaning, though she really felt like letting her heat out. Instead, she took deep breaths and focused her mind on seeking her prey through the store's labyrinth of aisles. Her eyes narrowed. Her face projected forward like that of a wolf tracking a hare's scent.

The man was out of sight now, vanished somewhere into the nebulous depths of the Cashstretch building. And for certain, it was a *large* store. Cashstretch—Make Your Bottom Dollar Go Further!— had only been in existence for three years, but it was doing its damnest to catch up with Walmart. In addition to this Worcester branch, the retail chain had twelve other branches across Massachusetts (including a monster outlet in the Boston suburb of West Roxbury), and was already making fast inroads down into Connecticut and up into New Hampshire, Vermont and Maine.

The point here was, that Cashstretch stocked practically everything there was to buy, which meant the young man with the perfect calves might take quite a while in getting back to Jane.

But what if, she wondered, *when he returns, he doesn't stop at my counter, but instead, steps 'next door' to Danielle's?*

Then she smirked. It didn't matter. She had her ways of getting what she wanted. During Jane's three years of working here at Cashstretch she'd devised an almost infallible system of securing the information she desired. All she needed was to be here at the counters when the young man pushed his shopping cart out of the aisles.

She wondered what he could be buying though—she checked her watch—it was now fifteen minutes since he'd entered the store.

She shrugged. The main problem was that she was due to go off-shift in twenty minutes. The young man should have come out by then. But, if he hadn't, all hope wasn't lost then either. She had two more options to snare him: she could either walk through the store on some pretext and chat him up, or hurry outside and 'bump into him' and chat him up as he carried his bags to his car.

A blonde woman in a black business suit stepped towards her. Pondering her huntress puzzle with half her mind, Jane attended to the woman.

Smiling, she bagged the blonde's cranberry juice and milk, then handed her her change and a receipt.

The blonde didn't smile back. Not out of nastiness: she merely seemed hassled and worried, and most of all, in a hurry to get somewhere. All the while Jane had been tallying up the cost of her purchases, she'd been staring at her wristwatch. She took her bag of drinks from Jane and hurried off.

"Next please." Then she froze. Next on her queue was the young man she'd been waiting for: the man with the perfect body. Here, next to her in the flesh, he was twice as good-looking as from a distance.

She wasn't really surprised that he'd chosen her counter. Not even though Tony had just arrived back from the restrooms and his cash register had been free all the while she'd been attending to the blonde. She glanced sideways at Tony. Yes, he'd definitely gone to either shoot up or sniff something—his eyes were much too bright, his pupils too large. Tony looked like his blue-and-orange Cashstretch uniform was propping him up and not the other way around.

She looked back at her young man—did he sense the same connection that she did? Did he realize that from this point on his life was inextricably entangled with hers? Or—she was always honest in her assessment of situations—had he simply felt that Tony's dilated eyes looked creepy, and stepped up to the 'hot redhead' next to him instead.

Though not in the least bit vain, Jane wasn't modest either in her assessment of her looks. She knew she was very attractive. And just like other attractive women did, she regularly used what she had to get what she wanted.

Just that in her case, what she wanted wasn't a work promotion or someone else's man.

Whatever the reasons for this young man's choosing her over her companion, he was here now. He was hers now. A fact that he wasn't in the least aware of.

She saw that he wasn't really paying attention to her as he loaded his purchases onto the counter. Maybe he had a girlfriend and was the faithful type; or maybe he was just in a hurry to get home and watch a football game.

Each movement he made flexed his perfectly developed muscles. She began feeling flushed and wet between her legs again. In between scanning and bagging his stuff, she wiped her forehead and found it covered with sweat.

Most of what he'd bought was health food stuff—organic cucumbers and radishes, energy bars and protein shakes and such like.

Yummy, maybe that's why his body looks so good! But the muscle development is all his own—he looks like he was born and raised in a gym.

He'd also bought some paperback novels, two bottles of red wine, and an electric razor.

"Will that be cash or charge, sir?"

He handed her his credit card. She glanced cursorily at it, taking in all the details before swiping it. His name was Robert Francis. She grinned, did the accounting, and handed the card back to him along with his receipt.

Now was the time. There wasn't anyone approaching behind Robert Francis. It seemed the stars had aligned themselves in her favor. In *their* favor.

She smiled at him. This was a different smile, a cold, calculating smile. It was a prostitute's smile. She'd rehearsed it till she'd gotten it perfect. She had different smiles for men and women. For men, she needed to be sexy but demure, attainable, but just slightly out of reach. With women, she needed to project camaraderie, the sense of 'we're all in this together' that assured them she understood their struggles and shared their aspirations.

"Well, thanks for shopping with us, sir," she said, handing him a glossy blue form. "I hope you don't mind filling this out?"

He took it from her, his massive arms flexing magnificently, and looked it over. "Win a cruise trip to the Bahamas?" He stared back at her. "What's this?"

Jane explained: "To reward our faithful customers, Cashstretch holds a promotional competition twice a year. The last one was for a trip to Hong Kong. This one's a 14-day cruise to the Bahamas." She was still smiling her siren's smile at him, willing him to want what she was offering because he subconsciously wanted her. She was like one of those magazine ads featuring a member of the opposite sex as subliminal bait to override the reader's purchasing inhibitions.

She knew what she was doing to him. She also knew he had no idea what she was doing to him.

"And I qualify?" he asked. "Just by shopping here?" He was waving the card in those perfect fingers. He ran his other hand through his straw-colored hair. His perfect legs were hidden by the counter and cash register, but Jane didn't mind that. She suspected she'd be seeing a whole lot of them in just a short while.

"Have you previously entered for this in any of our other branches?"

He shook his head. "Nope. First time I'm seeing or hearing of it."

She nodded. "You do qualify then. The competition is open to everyone who buys goods worth more than a hundred dollars at a time." She peered at the figure on the cash register. "At $139, you more than qualify."

He laughed. "Ah, but I'd better not, miss. I never seem to win anything. Each time I play poker with the guys, it's as though the odds of fate conspire against me to deal better cards to the other players."

He glanced down at the blue form, with its depiction of a joyful family of five on vacation, and below that, the six or seven dotted lines which awaited his answers to its questions, then outside toward his car—a silver SUV. Jane determined the SUV was his because it was the only vehicle in the area of the parking lot he was staring at which hadn't arrived in the last ten minutes. There had been a lot of vehicle turnaround in that area, but the silver SUV had doggedly resisted being persuaded to depart by its mechanical fellows, and had remained at its waiting post.

"Besides, I'm in a hell of a hurry," Robert Francis insisted in an almost pleading voice. He clearly wasn't interested in the competition but at the same time didn't wish to offend her. He looked behind him, to see if anyone was coming; such an interruption would give him a reason to leave her. No one was approaching who would enable him to depart without seeming rude. Danielle had a line of three in front of her, and Tony had five people waiting, but as though the roped-off lane to Jane's counter was peopled with visible ghosts, no one made the slightest attempt to step behind Robert Francis, or ask him to carry off his bags.

Jane felt anger at Robert then. He clearly hadn't yet understood that they were fated to be together.

Not that any of them ever did. This was more than some random encounter. It was *Fate*. It wasn't like she was stalking him; he was here of his own free will. This was more involved than her merely trespassing on another's personal space.

It was vitally important that he fill in the contest forms. Not for Cashstretch's benefit, but for Jane's.

He shook his head. "I'm sorry, I'm really not the travelling kind. I'm more of an armchair tourist."

She turned on the charm. "Aw, c'mon, sir, what harm can it possibly do?" She flashed him that evil disarming smile again, peeling away his half-hearted defense, blowing back his emotional resistance like a barrage of artillery shells. "And . . . the trip's actually for *four* people. You can take your girlfriend"—he wasn't wearing a wedding ring—"and two kids also."

He grinned. "Girlfriend? At the moment I don't have one . . . except of course, you're single."

She returned a sad smile at him. "No such luck. I'm taken, and he's a mean and jealous bastard too." She grinned. "But, hey—you never know—the draw's still four months off. Lots of time to hook up with Miss Right before then."

It worked. He nodded and took the form. "You know, you're right—my romantic luck *is* overdue for a change." He patted himself down, then asked, "Have you a pen I can borrow? I could take the card home and bring it in next week, but I live out of town and I'm certain to forget to return it once work catches up with me."

She almost didn't hear him; she was that delighted. *Yes!*

Then she quickly found him a pen. And waited.

She made idle talk while he filled in the form: "Your address has two uses, sir: First, it assures us that you actually qualify for the draw, which is only open to Massachusetts residents; and second"—she laughed coolly like she was sharing an intimate and private joke— "well, secondly, it also lets us know where to send the winning tickets to. Yeah, I know that's weird, 'cos usually we have a big presentation at the head office for the winners, complete with TV cameras and a big dinner and everything."

He handed her the filled form. She took it from him and reviewed what he'd written: *Robert Francis. 26 Glen Ellen Road, Paxton, MA 01612. Email address: robert.francis@maxsgymworld.com. Phone number . . .* Unknown to him, she had a photographic memory. Just as with his credit card, she immediately committed the entire address to memory.

She looked back up at him, smiling the same deadly smile that had hooked him and made him hers. "This is just fine, sir." She handed the form back to him and pointed towards the store entrance. "Please, slip it into the contest bin—the blue one right beside the door."

After a final disarming smile from Jane, Robert Francis left, thinking what a charming woman she was, and also planning a future visit to Worcester specifically to drop in here at Cashstretch to talk to her.

As he strode off with this twin shopping bags, Jane admired his fantastic physique again. He had a nice butt too, but his calves were what she liked best about him.

She watched him drop the contest form into its bin, then turned to attend to a middle-aged woman who'd begun placing canned fruit on the counter.

"Hello, Mrs. Beasley," she greeted. "How's everything going this week?"

She fell into idle chit-chat with the woman, and a few minutes later her shift at the cash register was over. Maria Hernandez relieved her at her station and she was off and able to plan her next moves.

***

"You really liked that guy, didn't you?" Danielle asked while they both changed out of their uniforms in the ladies' changing room.

Jane turned to face the woman. "Huh? Which guy?" Danielle was small, with big blue eyes and a snub nose. Now that she was supposedly pregnant, Jane expected her to double in size again like she had last time.

Danielle pulled a sweater down over her head before slyly replying: "That last guy you served, the cute one who was all muscles that you convinced to enter the cruise contest. I was watching you from the corner of my eyes. You really digged him, didn't you?"

Jane shrugged and played along. She posed saucily. "And . . . what if I did?"

Danielle giggled. "Scott wouldn't like it, for one thing."

Laughing, Jane pulled off her sneakers. She indeed remembered how turned on the man in question had gotten her. "Girl, let *me* worry about what Scotty likes. Besides, there's no harm in a woman just *looking*, is there? I haven't seen a hunk that well-built in ages. Did you see his six-pack?"

"Oh, I sure did, girlfriend. It was more like an eight-or-ten pack though."

Danielle had replied in a near-whisper. Melanie and Fatima, two of the other women who'd just left the checkout counters, were also in changing room, though Fatima was wearing headphones and wouldn't hear anything they said. Melanie too was preoccupied: she was on the phone to her boyfriend. But both women knew Danielle's husband Jerry and Danielle didn't want to seed any catty gossip that could cause trouble for her at home.

"I'm just saying," Danielle said. "Janie, you were licking your lips like you couldn't wait to suck that guy off."

Her comment startled Jane. *I lost that much self-control?* While zipping up her jacket, she made a cold mental note to keep better check on her emotions in future. Then she shrugged off Danielle's comment.

"I'm ovulating," she whispered conspiratorially to the other woman. "At the moment, even the sight of a banana gets me wet."

Danielle burst out laughing. "Don't I know it, girl."

Jane went on: "Girl, tonight, Scott won't know what hit him in bed. He'll be nursing the bruises on his rod for months to come."

***

Jane and Danielle left the department store together, walking around the building to the staff parking lot where Danielle was parked.

Jane turned down the ride home Danielle offered her. She had her own car (she had two vehicles actually), but hardly ever drove to work. The half-mile walk to and fro kept her in shape, kept her strong and alert. Those minutes spent in foot transit were also a good time to think and strategize.

Walking also meant that she didn't have to look into a car's rearview mirrors. Jane had a thing about mirrors. A bad thing, as in she *hated* them. Even now, standing beside Danielle's white Honda, she'd intentionally positioned herself by the hood rather than the driver's door, so that she was in front of the side mirror and didn't have to look at it. Even an accidental glance wasn't acceptable.

"Say, Janie," Danielle said after buckling her seatbelt. "Did you hear what Tony said?"

"What'd he say?" She wasn't really interested in knowing. She wanted to get a move on towards home. She had a lot to think about.

"Well," Danielle explained, "he said he saw *something* while relieving himself in the men's room."

"What kind of a something?" While asking the question, Jane's eyes swept back toward their workplace. The Cashstretch building looked like a cream-colored aircraft hangar besieged by an invading army.

Danielle now looked both confused and a little frightened. "That's the weird thing. He says he didn't see it for long enough to be sure, but that it looked like a man's shadow, only a weirdly distorted one."

Jane laughed but didn't say anything, so Danielle went on: "He said there was no one else in the men's room at the time, just himself, and that the shadow fell over him while he was washing his hands. He thought that maybe either Adam or José had walked in—he'd met them both outside in the hallway on his way in—but on turning around, he discovered he was still all alone in the lavatory and that the door was shut."

Jane looked amused. "A moving, detached shadow in the toilet? That sounds almost like a ghost story."

"It's creepy though," Danielle said with a slight shiver. "I hate how he said the shadow was all distorted-like, not human at all."

Jane laughed. "You bet. Danni, Tony was most likely stoned and hallucinated the whole incident. Either that or he's just pranking everyone. I, for one, refuse to believe for a second that Cashstretch now has a ghost. And in the daytime?"

Danielle pondered on that a moment. Then she nodded. "Yeah, I guess you're right. You know, one of these days Mr. Ackerman is gonna catch him getting high, and he'll be out the back door . . . or worse . . ."

Jane nodded. 'Or worse' clearly meant Cashstretch management handing Tony Marler over to the police for prosecution and possible incarceration. She shrugged. "It'll be his fault if he gets busted like that. I've told him twice already that if he wants to do recreational drugs, to do them at home, but he won't listen to me."

Danielle nodded. She said her goodbyes to Jane, then drove off.

Jane watched her go for a moment, then, pulling her coat tightly around her, she turned and strode off towards home, crossing the parking lot to Stafford Street.

The Cashstretch store was situated in Worcester's Webster Square neighborhood, up near the top end of Stafford Street where it joined Main Street, and a hundred or so yards across the road from Curtis Ponds.

Jane lived half a mile away, down on Grandview Avenue.

After a few paces she got out her phone and plugged in some earphones.

Slain Jane. The new *Bitch Perfect* album, though she still detested that slutty cover. The stacked layers of digitally polished noise in her ears helped her ignore the polished, reflective glass storefronts she passed. She wasn't about looking at herself, no matter what.

Between her ears, Janet Orgasm crooned:

"Yeah, so I met this guy that I really liked,
And I took him home for the ride of his life.
Oh, it turned out he was really nice,
We ate each other all through the night,
Yeah, we both really worked up quite an appetite."

Jane Winters liked that particular verse. *Worked up quite an appetite.* It put her in mind of her own peculiar hobby. Wistfully, her thoughts went to the man she'd met at work today. Robert Francis. Was he expecting her to call on him? Of course he wasn't. Did he imagine what was about happening to him? Of course he didn't. None of them ever did. She was like Fate, a random occurrence that would pick his front door to knock on.

But it wasn't happening yet. She'd have liked to visit him tonight—once again she felt that familiar rush of blood in her groin, padding and expanding her private parts out to a juicy erotic fullness—but she had principles as to how she operated. She always left at least a two-week interval between cause and effect. Sometimes (for instance, if Mr. Francis returned to shop in Cashstretch again before the requisite fortnight was up, and he and she chatted) she might even let the waiting period extend to a month or two.

Never must there be even the slightest suggestion of any connection between herself and the misfortune which befell her victims.

So she'd wait. *I'm the patient dog who eats the fattest bone. I'm more patient than a buzzard.*

The similes brought a smile to her lips. But then she remembered what Danielle had said about Tony. A frown replaced her smile as she trod the evening sidewalk between shoppers and those others, who like herself were ending their workday.

So, Tony's seeing things, is he? Well, I need to keep an eye on him to ensure he doesn't see things he shouldn't.

CHAPTER 4

Jane, Augmented...

Janet Mary Winters was several things which she didn't in the least look like:

***

First of all, Jane was a genius. She had an IQ of 189. This had been tested while she was in high school, but neither she nor her guardians at the time (her Uncle Charlie and Aunt Margaret) had taken the results seriously. Neither had anyone at school, where Jane had previously shown no signs of brilliance whatsoever. As a high-schooler, Jane had consistently excelled at being average, getting D's in everything except mathematics and biology, where she got consistent B's.

Jane's teachers had assumed her IQ test results to be a fluke, except if they proved her to be a genius at mediocrity.

In this supposition, her teachers were much more correct than they could have imagined: Jane was intentionally getting medium scores so as not to attract any attention to herself. She didn't want to stand out from the crowd. Once she'd hit puberty, she'd had a weird sense of a greater purpose that she was meant to fulfill, one which wouldn't be served by her being popular. So she'd surfed at mid-tide, doing just enough to get out of high school with a chance of going to college if she wanted to. Many times she'd been tempted to dazzle everyone with her brilliance—every single exam she'd ever sat for was so simple it made her laugh—but then, on remembering that strange 'future purpose' which she increasing felt pulling on her but which she couldn't yet even guess the nature of, she'd always cautioned herself and written just enough to give her a basic pass in the subjects, intentionally writing wrong answers to several questions.

Since reaching adulthood, Jane had taken ten online IQ tests, in none of which she'd scored less that 187. Just like with her high school examinations, she found the tests ridiculously easy.

She took it in her stride. Having an exceptional mind made her activities much easier; it helped her to plan better and control situations. Yes, even in exceptional, unexpected circumstances Jane found it easy to assume control. This might only be a subtle control, might consist merely of managing her own reaction to a sudden crises, but the control was definitely there. Jane Winters was colder than ice, she never, ever panicked.

Yes, Jane was a very brainy woman.

***

Secondly, Jane Winters was great at self-defense. Most of this was self-taught, though she'd also taken several judo courses.

Jane was also much stronger than she looked.

Of recent, Jane had been instructing herself in the art of 'hono,' an ancient system of incapacitating one's opponent by means of a series of touches to the body's pressure points. She'd found the information online and was still determining its effectiveness in practical situations.

So far, hono seemed genuine, something she could use. A week ago, in the Cashstretch ladies' toilets, Jane had successfully put Roxanne Bailey to sleep. All it had taken was a little firm pressure on the back of Roxanne's neck.

At the time, they'd been discussing their supervisor, Mr. Ackerman.

Roxanne had been preoccupied with fixing her makeup before they both went out to the cash registers. She'd been bent forward over a sink and staring into its mirror bug-eyed. She hadn't thought anything of Jane's offering to help her straighten out her tangled hair.

She'd also not questioned Jane's explanation a few moments later, as to why she was holding her up and splashing water in her face.

"You fainted," Jane had said, holding Roxanne in such a way that she didn't have to look in the mirror herself. "I managed to catch you before you hit the floor."

Of course, Roxanne had agreed with Jane. On her part, she'd suddenly felt inexplicably woozy, as if a fist had squeezed her brain.

She'd thanked Jane for her help, and then, once her feet felt firm under her again, had gotten right back to work fixing her makeup.

Jane was a very cunning woman.

***

Thirdly, Jane Winters was a sociopath. Though on the surface she looked wholesome and was friendly and calm, in reality she was crazier than Christmas in a cramped two-bedroom bungalow when one's entire extended family came visiting.

Since becoming an adult woman and finally understanding what that long simmering unknown 'purpose' of her life was, Jane had never once considered herself crazy. She was merely 'different'—that was all. She didn't think herself more highly evolved than other people. But then, neither did she see herself as an atavist. She was simply *herself*, and if she fit a certain unpleasant psychological profile, so be it.

Yes, Jane was well aware of how a psychiatrist would view her activities. She knew he'd call her 'nuts,' but that didn't bother her any. She accepted her difference from everyone else. In a sense, she celebrated her deviancy. She did what she did, and she did it safely, both for herself and her victims.

She knew she would never be caught. Not dead, not alive. She was an ant in a catacomb, a single leaf in a forest, a grain of sand in the desert—impossible to find. By shrewd, calculating steps (like working an obscure low-paying job in a supermarket when she could instead be earning megabucks stock-trading or fashion modeling), she'd arranged things perfectly to suit her pursuits.

To Jane's mind, she still walked on the 'genius' side of the divide between 'genius' and 'crazy.' It was only the mad who made mistakes.

Other than for just one aspect of her life, she felt she was a perfectly normal woman.

Despite knowing she wasn't crazy, Jane would have loved to see a psychiatrist anyway. Because of the thing about the mirrors. Maybe a shrink could help her weird phobia. But she'd never visited one, because at some point in the consultation he might want to hypnotize her, and knowing what she sometimes did in her free time, she couldn't have anyone poking around in her subconscious mind.

She'd decided she'd just have to endure it. Like everyone else, she had no choice but to live with herself.

At least she had an excellent mind. A mind that billions of people around the world would give their right arms or legs to own.

This of course, was Jane's personal and very biased opinion. Just as no one can see the back of their own head (an act that's difficult even using mirrors), Jane's opinion of her mental state was her own blind spot.

But, by everyone else's definition of the word, Jane Winters was clinically insane.

***

All in all, Janet Mary Winters was a very, very, very, very, very, very, very, very, very, very dangerous woman.

CHAPTER 5

Robert...three weeks later...

Rob Francis came awake slowly. Really, he was half-awake, hovering at the edge of consciousness like a nightmare uncertain if it wanted to scare the dreamer.

But tonight, even being half-awake felt extra-strange to Rob.

His head felt as if he was due a hangover, only the hangover hadn't yet found the right nerve cords to yank on to announce its presence. Like he'd taken an overdose of sleeping pills but hadn't been able to die. He felt weak, enervated. A dull pain pricked his lungs. His tongue felt swollen and oddly dry. Waking up hurt mysteriously.

But, I only had two beers with Stephenie . . . Stephenie Bower was the girl he'd had dinner with. First date. They both worked for Max's Gym World, a manufacturer of gym and fitness equipment. Stephenie was cute and intelligent and he intended asking her out again as soon as possible.

Rob's next surprise came when he discovered he was lying face-down in bed. He never slept face-down, and had never once woken up in that position either. The best explanation he could think of was that he'd had a nightmare of some kind.

Then it got worse. Attempting to turn over in bed, Rob found he couldn't move his left arm. It felt totally numbed. No, that was wrong. It wasn't his entire arm that seemed dead, just the forearm. He could sense his upper arm as a distinct part of himself, but from the elbow down, he had no sensation whatsoever. His right arm, however, felt perfectly normal.

What the . . . ?

Rob had just discovered that he had exactly the same lack of sensation in both of his legs. Both felt truncated at the knees.

Up till this point, Rob had lurked on the blurry edges of sleep, unwilling to exit Dreamland and then have to pay the time-toll for reentry. He'd have willingly attributed the odd numbness in his left forearm to an extreme case of pins-and-needles caused by the unfamiliar sleeping position in which he'd woken. The arm didn't hurt and could be overlooked; the legs less so, but then, seeing as he didn't really want to wake up—his mind felt soothed by a comforting liquidity, as if it was itself a sleeper and had just had pillows plumped under its head—he just might be able to nod off again. It would take some work, sure; but, given just the right lack of mental insistence, he should be able to swing it.

But then Rob discovered something else that was really troubling: The bed felt wet.

Have I peed on myself? This also was something Rob had never done before; not even in college, where he'd gotten inebriated on a regular basis. Even when shitfaced and unable to walk straight, he had great bladder control.

I only had those two beers.

He tried feeling around himself for the wetness, but with his left arm refusing to work he could really only tell for certain that there was no wetness on his right side. The wetness appeared to be located under his left upper arm and side, and also lower down his body, around his groin and legs. So yes, it might have been urine, but if it was, how then had it spread up to his arms, rather than just soaking away into the mattress?

An owl hooted outside. Its noise shattered Rob's dreamy state. The owl's cry jerked him up over the threshold of consciousness, so that there was no chance of him falling asleep again. Besides, by now lying on his belly had begun feeling damned uncomfortable.

So now, Rob was forced to take cognizance of why he seemed unable to turn himself over. To do this though, he first *had to* turn himself over. Doing so wasn't impossible, but could apparently only be accomplished now by pushing with his right hand and both knees. But Rob Francis was a strong and very muscular young man, and he got it done.

By the time he'd got himself turned over and sitting up, Rob was very alarmed. In fact, he was scared as hell. Heart pounding, he reached over to the nightstand and flicked on the bedside light.

Then he sat there propped up against the headboard and gaped at himself. The narcotic or whatever he'd been drugged with swum through his mind like a shark eating the very pain it had caused him.

For a long moment, Rob imagined that maybe, just maybe, he was still dreaming. What he was seeing just didn't seem possible.

He was sitting in a bloodstained bed. That in itself was crazy enough. But what was crazier still was the state of his body:

Someone had stripped all the skin and flesh off his left forearm and off both of his legs below the knees. No, the limbs/extremities hadn't be amputated, but they might just as well have been: all that remained below his elbow and knees were red bones. All the flesh of his left hand was similarly missing, but both his feet were still normal.

Expertly applied tourniquets adorned his upper arm and thighs; two on each limb. None of his ghastly wounds was bleeding or even dribbling. Nor was there an excessive amount of blood splattered on the bed. Most of the bleeding was localized; the blood that had wet his boxer shorts had dribbled inward down his left thigh to reach its destination.

Rob sat motionless and took all this in. He was frozen by disbelief, trapped in a moment in time; a victim of a nightmare which he'd somehow freed from the dream realm and dragged into his waking reality.

My arm? My legs? Who the hell fucking did this to me? How? How?

He realized that for someone to have butchered him like this, they'd have needed to drug him first and then take their time with the surgery.

He had no idea when he began crying, hot tears welling from his eyes. He'd been ruined. His perfect body was ruined. His entire life was ruined. His job, his love life . . . everything he'd had had just gone up in smoke.

He sat there confused, without a sensible thought in his head. Nothing could ever prepare one for the horror of waking up with important parts of one's body missing.

Rob was still weeping when he noticed the large white card on the nightstand. It had a large red message printed on it:

Call 911, the message read.

More confused than ever now, unable to stop himself from bawling like a baby, Rob Francis began feeling around himself for his cellphone.

CHAPTER 6

Jane

At 3.27 a.m., about the exact time when in the neighboring town of Paxton, perplexed paramedics were loading the still-weeping Rob Francis into their ambulance, back home in Worcester, Jane Winters was loading the meat she'd carved off Rob's body into a freezer in her basement. (She had three top-of-the-range freezers down there, one of which was merely on standby in case either of the others broke down.)

With a dreamy smile on her face, she transferred the meat from the black icebox she always carried on such assignments into five Ziploc bags, and then stashed the bags alongside several similar frozen packages.

While transferring Rob's leg skin into its own Ziploc bag, Jane licked her lips in anticipation. Yes, she'd taken his skin as well. It wasn't just that she liked the taste of fried or roasted human skin, but that also, seeing as she'd removed all the blood vessels between Rob's knees and ankles, both of his lower legs would certainly need to be amputated, and then the skin would wind up going to waste. The same went for his arm. To Jane, wasting such a delicacy was an unforgiveable crime. She had however left sufficient skin in place to dress each resulting stump with.

She smiled at her collection of raw meat. She considered herself a genius of human science, a mistress of the art of human resources management.

Once done putting her fresh edibles away, Jane shut the freezer, filled the empty cooler with soapy water, and turned off the basement lights. Shutting the basement door behind her, she climbed the stairs to the main house.

It had been a wonderful trip out of town, but she really needed to get some sleep. She was working the first shift and hated being late.

At the top of the basement stairs, Jane slid the access panel back into place, checked that it was properly locked, then crossed the hallway and headed upstairs to bed.

***

No one but Jane knew that her house still had a basement. On moving back into this building—her parents' old two-story residence on Grandview Avenue—she'd immediately taken steps to conceal the basement's existence from prying eyes.

The cellar entrance was in the hallway, almost opposite the broom closet, and had been built as a continuation of the stairs that descended from the second floor. Jane had repaneled the entire hallway with dark wood, leaving a removable section in front of the basement door. This portion slid open only when she entered a passcode into a combination lock cunningly concealed in its top. And once shut, it was impossible to distinguish from the rest of the hallway woodwork.

Once these modifications had been made, Jane had informed her Aunt Margaret and Uncle Charlie (who both knew the house's original layout) that she'd had the basement filled in because it was weakening the house's foundations.

After that, she'd begun moving her tools downstairs. Freezers, scalpels and cleavers, a portable meat grinder . . .

CHAPTER 7

Ghost

Onscreen. Two beautiful and naked girls wearing high heels in bed, one with her fingers in the other's vagina. Both girls covered in sweat. Both panting loudly for the camera, their gasps and moans creating an extra layer of erotic stimulation.

Fast forward.

The blonde arranges the brunette on her hands and knees, then kneeling behind her, begins tonguing her anus. It's quite a gaping anus, looks extremely well visited by penises. The blonde sticks two fingers into the open anus and swirls them about. It's porn, meaning of course that there's no feces in sight—this isn't that sort of video. The blonde's other hand sneaks down to the brunette's vagina and starts rubbing vigorously.

Fast forward again.

The brunette pushes back against the penetrating fingers, moans "Fuck me!" and then gasps that she's coming. Juice squirts from her sex. Seeing the pale gush, the blonde instantly inverts herself so she's lying on her back with her mouth positioned under the other girl's vagina. She starts drinking the squirting liquid, while still rubbing and penetrating her lover.

Fast forward.

The movie fades to black, then resumes at another scene: a man pissing in the blonde's open mouth, while she does her best not to let a drop of it spill from her lips. "Hey, you'd better not mess up my makeup," she jokes after a quick swallow, while he urinates in her hair instead. Across the room, the brunette is sitting on a leather couch, masturbating and licking her lips, her blue eyes full of desire for either the penis or the urine coming out of it.

***

Ghost clicked the movie off. Wrong one again. It definitely wasn't *Squirting and Pee-Drinking Bitches 9*. The film had looked promising at the start though.

She was about closing the video window, but decided to 'favorite' and tag it instead. This film reminded her of a request she'd had about a year ago; she'd look into that later. She stored the movie in the appropriate Firefox folder, closed it, then opened the next one. As this fresh porno rolled its opening credits, she ran the 'find' info through her mind:

It's an old film, early 2000's when I saw it, but I don't recall which year. From the performers' accents, I'd hazard a guess that it's either Canadian or English. A blonde and brunette lesbian scene. They don't really say anything until the end, when one girl tells the other: "Great way to kill time, huh?" That final statement is about the only thing I really remember. Oh yeah, I also think one of the girls squirts.

***

Two other girls fucking in bed, both blondes this time, though one has short hair. Short Hair has Long Hair on her back and is sixty-nining her.

Fast forward.

Tongues lustily slurping sexes, fingers dipping into wet holes. Smeared lipstick. Spit on cheeks and chins. Short Hair inserts more fingers into Long Hair. Long Hair's eyes gape open wide . . .

Fast forward.

Long Hair has Short Hair on her hands and knees. Doggy style with a strap-on. Both girls sweating bullets. Short Hair's mouth gaping like she's either in agony or ecstasy. She's feeling something anyhow.

Fast forward toward the end. Neither girl squirts, but still, listen carefully.

This time both young women just giggle a lot then argue over who's going to prepare breakfast.

It clearly isn't this one either: both blondes have American accents.

***

Ghost closed the video then rubbed her eyes. She got up from her desk and stretched. Then she went to make herself some instant coffee.

Ghost was an athletically built young woman of average height. She was twenty-six. She was a brunette, with similarly dark eyes and a prominent nose that she intended having fixed once she had enough money.

Standing there in her panties in the kitchenette of her studio apartment while waiting for the kettle to boil, she pondered this search request. It was simple enough, but there were literally thousands of videos to look through.

It helps a bit that he's narrowed it down with his 'either British or Canadian' reference, but still . . .

The water boiled. She heaped spoons of coffee into her large mug, then heaped in equally large amounts of sugar. A lot of milk too. She tasted the coffee, decided it was both sweet and 'coffee' enough, then got a bar of chocolate out of her fridge and went back into her bedroom.

It was midnight now. Wednesday had just become Thursday. Coffee mug in hand, Ghost walked to her apartment window and stared out over the city of Worcester. She was high up on Front Street, right in the middle of the city. She regarded the spread tapestry of house lights below her. She imagined the lives those lights indicated. Lots of people sleeping or fucking. Happiness, love. Babies being conceived.

For a moment she felt sad that this wasn't her own life too. But, different strokes for different folks, right? And it wasn't as if anyone had chosen her life for her. She enjoyed the life she led.

She returned to her work desk. Her favorite laptop had in the meantime gone to sleep. She woke it up again and got back to work. As usual, she'd get to sleep at around 4 a.m. But before then, she had about a hundred porn videos to skim through.

The money was great though. This guy was offering $500 for her to locate this obscure flick for him.

***

Ghost found things for people. Not in the real world; in the virtual one. She ran an internet 'Find' service. For a fee she located stuff for people that they didn't have either the time or the patience or knowhow to look for themselves.

She got requests to unearth all sorts of stuff: software, music, books, films. She'd been surprised at how willing people were to pay her to trawl through search engines, YouTube, eBay, forums and torrent sites, and other really obscure and mostly unknown places on their behalves. It paid well and meant she didn't have to work at Subway or McDonalds.

Most of the time, the people who hired Ghost simply couldn't remember the name of what they were looking for. They'd maybe seen it in passing somewhere, or watched it on TV when they were little kids, or read it as teenagers, and now as adults no one they asked could tell them what it was called.

But they felt a need to relive that long-ago experience. And Ghost provided it for them.

Oddly enough, she got less requests to find porn than she'd thought she might. On average, she only got one or two requests for those each month. Most of those were like this present case: a video from twenty years ago which the man (or woman—everyone used avatars and screen names now; gender was less predictable that the stock exchange) clearly felt nostalgic about for some reason.

Also, whoever had hired her to find this old lesbian flick was clearly wealthy; he'd paid upfront without negotiating. She'd told him it might take her a month to locate the movie. If by then she'd not found it, she'd return half of the money to him, keeping the other half as her search fee. No problem, he'd responded.

Most jobs she got were as harmless as this. She never bothered to respond to requests asking her to find child porn. And weirdly, no one had yet requested that she find bestiality for them. Either no one was ever nostalgic about that sort of sexual experience, or the modern internet more than satisfied their needs.

Ghost did, however, regularly get requests to find *people*. Or rather, to find out how 'genuine' people were. These were mostly to resolve romantic issues, coming from women and men who were scared they were being duped by online lovers using fake dating profiles.

Other people used Ghost to locate people from their pasts who didn't use social media. She was some kind of online private detective. Sometimes it was dark and sleazy work. But then, Ghost didn't mind sleaze.

Ghost fast-forwarded through thirty more videos of beautiful women bringing each other to orgasm, then decided to take a break. Amongst other things, watching all that sexual intercourse was getting her turned on, and she wasn't ready to have an orgasm just yet. Despite all the caffeine in her system, sex would relax her. Relaxation meant sleep, and sleep meant not working. Not working meant no money. And like everyone else on the 3rd planet, Ghost needed money, which meant no masturbation till she was through working.

But, hey!—she did need a mental breather. She closed the media player and pulled up OTTmeet instead.

***

OTTmeet was Facebook for eccentrics and freaks. The web layout even looked like Facebook, with friend invites and notifications and 'likes' (and in this case 'dislikes' too), and with each user having a personal timeline on which they could post whatever they liked so long as it was legal.

On OTTmeet, privacy was key. Everyone used screen names and avatars. The site hosted multiple chatrooms and there were lots of online clubs that members could join.

Sex, violence, humor . . . everything was catered for, the more 'over the top' the better. OTTmeet took over where 'polite' and 'well-behaved' social media platforms like Instagram and Twitter left off.

"You wanna get Freaky? Welcome to OTTmeet!" was the site's proud boast. And it did its best to live up to it.

It was fun.

Ghost was a member of several OTTmeet clubs. In particular, she was an avid participant in the BDSM Safe Word club.

A notification beeped. Anna Jeisen had just posted more pictures of her cats. Ghost knew Anna: the woman was a wealthy middle-aged divorcee with too much time on her hands. Last year Ghost had helped Anna Jeisen locate two obscure 70's adventure films set in Chile.

Since then they'd kept in touch, chatting occasionally. One of their chats had revealed that they both shared an interest in BDSM culture, though Anna was wary of joining any of the OTTmeet BDSM groups.

She'd written: *Count me out, baby. Too much chance of my picking up some crazy whose idea of an S&M experience is him chainsawing you in the boobs and expecting you to moan in ecstasy while he's doing it.*

Too right, Ghost had responded. *But I can tell you from personal experience that Safe Word is okay.*

I'll think on it, Anna had replied, but as far as Ghost could see, Mrs. Jeisen hadn't yet worked up the nerve to join Safe Word.

So Anna Jeisen had a taste for hedonism, but lacked the courage to take a deep plunge. They'd exchanged photos. Anna Jeisen was very attractive; a perfectly groomed forty-five years old. A green-eyed blonde with big natural breasts a little distended from suckling two kids.

Seeing those photos, Ghost, who was bisexual, had thought that she'd very much enjoy planting her lips on Anna's vagina and licking her to orgasm.

Like Ghost, Anna also lived in Massachusetts, but over in Springfield. But Anna was a mouse, a woman who appeared terrified of social contacts outside of her rich and polite circles.

Ghost had suggested that they meet up: *For lunch and other things. You never know what might happen. You might like it.*

But Anna hadn't wanted them to hook up and possibly make love to each other. She'd cooled down their online relationship after that suggestion.

Ghost hadn't really minded. She had lots to do. Lots of people and stuff to find. And besides, she wasn't really desperate for sex. Safe Word more than kept her satisfied. The club had regular 'In The Flesh' nights where members met in person and got their freak on.

But Ghost still kept up her contact with Anna, who, once it was clear that the younger woman wasn't going to insist that they meet up in person, became very willing to chat with her again.

Mostly they chatted about everyday things. From their discussions, Ghost had the clear impression that Anna Jeisen was the prototype from which airheads were made. The woman was all looks and no brains. Perfect reality show material. Sometimes Ghost wondered why they were still friends.

But she always had the same answer to her own question: she kept imagining what it would be like to suck on those big breasts of Anna's. Those breasts seemed worth waiting for.

***

Ghost 'liked' Anna's latest cat-post, then clicked on the Safe Word icon. This opened up a new browser tab that showed a chained and naked man onto whose back a woman in black leather was whipping a bloody star.

Ghost entered her password into the inset login window and clicked 'Enter.'

Once she'd been granted admittance, she had a quick look around to see what was new. She couldn't loiter here: in addition to having work to finish, there was also the fact that browsing through Safe Word posts always got her sexually aroused.

She clicked over to the club notice board. Yes, there would be a *Safe Word—In The Flesh* meeting this Saturday night. Usual time and venue.

That was all she needed to know.

Pleased, Ghost logged out of Safe Word, minimized OTTmeet, then got up again. She needed to cool down, not from physical heat, but from the sexual fire she already felt building in her from anticipation of the coming *In The Flesh* meeting.

She lay in bed and stared at the ceiling till she felt calmer. Then she returned to her task of locating vintage porn.

***

Twelve videos into her search, Ghost received a OTTmeet message from her friend Ninja.

TULIP meeting this Saturday to discuss the latest developments, he'd written.

She grimaced. Why the hell did it have to be scheduled for Saturday?

She typed: *Online chat or in the flesh?*

In the flesh, spooky babe, Ninja typed back. *Face to face. That way we'll be sure everyone's paying attention. You know like I do, that Warrior's a Neanderthal throwback—utterly crap with modern technology: online chatting with him is like giving an orangutan a cellphone. Also, I want Playboy where I can see him; else there's likely to be some bimbo giving him a hand job or blow job at the same time as we're chatting. So . . . we'll meet here at my place. 7 p.m. prompt.*

She shook her head at the screen and typed back: *Hey, Ninja, do this for me, wilya? Let's meet here at my place instead. And make it 6 p.m., not 7. I need to be somewhere important later that night. Too much hassle for me to drive to yours and back afterwards to get ready.*

After the slight pause that meant Ninja was making up his mind on her request, the reply came in: *Okay, 6 p.m. your place it is. But make sure to fill your fridge with beers for the guys.*

She grinned at the screen. *Cool. There'll be as much booze as you want. Love to chat more but I'm busy tracking now. See ya on Sat night.*

That settled, she resumed her search.

***

Two hours, three cups of coffee, and eighty-seven videos later, Ghost found what she was looking for.

Busty Bavarian Backdoor Beauties. Country of origin: Germany. Date of Production: 2003.

The scene was almost exactly as her client had described it: two Scandinavian beauties in bed, licking and sucking each other and finally pleasuring themselves with strap-ons. The brunette of the pair squirting. Then afterwards, the blonde kissing the brunette and whispering that identifying line: "Great way to kill time, huh?"

Her client had however left out the most relevant part of the description—both women in the video clip had massive breasts.

Ghost tagged and saved the video, then got out a conveniently placed vibrator from a drawer in her work desk. After all that hard work, she figured she'd masturbate awhile to *Busty Bavarian Backdoor Beauties.* Those massive lesbian breasts had her really turned on.

She dildoed herself to several orgasms, imagining she was licking Anna Jeisen's vagina while some faceless man pumped her from behind.

CHAPTER 8

Jane

At work on a warm but rainy Saturday.

It was a week now since Jane had visited Robert Francis. As she tended to do each time, for the first couple of days after that visit she'd kept a keen eye and ear on the news, then lost interest.

The cops could investigate all they liked. They'd never find her.

She was a goddess among mortals.

Once again Jane was working the first shift. People and carts, more people and carts. Different faces with similar expressions and similar faces with different expressions.

Jane enjoyed the ebb and flow of customers. She liked looking at people's faces. She never got bored with that. She regarded each man and woman the way little children regard ice cream—as something that there can't ever be too much of. It was an additional perk to working at Cashstretch. The first perk, of course being that this cashier's job facilitated her hunt for fresh meat.

She didn't need this job. Along with the house, her parents had left her some money. And even if they hadn't left her any inheritance, she was brainy enough to get rich on her own. But, in another sense, she *did* need this job. It was perfect camouflage. She mustn't stand out; that was important. She must blend in with everyone else, must be as ordinary as they were, so that her extraordinary doings wouldn't ever be suspected.

And it was working. Working really well.

***

At around two-thirty that afternoon, two girls pushed loaded shopping carts up to Jane's checkout counter. The front cart was filled with bottles of wine and packs of beer, bar garnishes, sodas, and paper towels. The rear cart was piled high with frozen pizzas, large packs of chips and sandwich meats; bread, cheese, dips and assorted snacks, and boxes of candy bars and cookies. Jane had earlier noticed both young women in the drinks section of the store. They'd been arguing a lot.

Jane gave both young women a fast once-over. They were sisters, no doubts about that. The one in front was younger by about three years. The one in back was shorter and had a loud strident voice; she'd seemed to be the instigator in their quarrels. Both girls wore identical clothes—jeans jackets over T-shirts and jeans skirts over black leggings. Ankle boots. The only difference was in their hair: the front girl had short blonde hair, while her older sister's hair was long and black. Seeing as both girls' eyebrows matched their hair color, Jane assumed they hadn't dyed their hair, but that this was how they'd arrived from the womb.

The amount of drinks the sisters were purchasing meant they were throwing a party.

At first, Jane merely studied the sisters peripherally. Neither of them was meaty enough to hold her interest. (The younger sister had nice breasts, but Jane still had two sets of breasts in one of her basement freezers that she'd not yet gotten around to eating.) She concentrated on tallying up their purchases.

But then, after she'd gotten through summing the cost of all the drinks and the younger sister was helping the older one load the food they were buying onto the counter, Jane got a good look at the older one's face.

And then, all of a sudden the 'urge' was on her again.

Oh, there's something about her that I really like.

She took a good look to make sure the effort would be worth the payoff. Her exceptional mind kicked into overdrive. This older girl had high cheekbones and large lips. Her nose was small. She wasn't pretty, her face was too fleshy for that; but it was that fleshiness that now held Jane captivated. When the girl spoke, her lips and cheeks moved in a certain way that Jane found enthralling.

Jane felt a confirming rush of adrenalin. *Yes, I'll have some of this one!*

She had a quick look at the girl's left hand. No wedding ring. She felt relieved. A husband could prove to be a complication. Not because she couldn't incapacitate the man, but because it would be extra work—she already had these two women to deal with. Both sisters clearly lived together: "On the day of the party, we'll keep the champagne in your room so Donny doesn't drink it all up," the younger had said. 'Donny' might be either boyfriend or brother, but was most likely just a friend who was a lush. Every party had those.

Also, the similarity of their clothes meant one of them was wearing the other's wardrobe.

Jane made up her mind to visit the pair.

After that decision, everything else was easy. The sisters' final bill came to $328.24. The name on the older girl's credit card was Megan Morgan. The younger sister was called Karen.

Of course, they more than qualified for the Bahamas Cruise contest. Once Megan had signed her receipt, Jane pointed this out in an casual manner. Since deciding she liked Megan's face, she'd withdrawn a little, made certain to not be noticed showing more than a cashier's interest in her.

Karen was very pleased to hear about the contest. "Another one so soon?" she asked. "You had one in February, didn't you?"

"We do them twice a year," Jane explained. "More fun for our customers that way."

Karen shook her sister's arm. "Fill it in; we just might win."

Megan caught something of her sister's enthusiasm. She quickly filled in the contest form and handed it back for Jane to check. Jane read through it and memorized the pair's address. After returning the form to Megan, she helped the girls refill their shopping carts with their bagged purchases.

As they wheeled their carts away en route to the parking lot, Jane took one last look at Megan's wonderfully meaty face.

She looks delicious.

She felt intense delight and anticipation. She'd be visiting them shortly.

***

On her walk home from work that evening, Jane pondered how she'd felt in the store today. That rush of desire to possess Megan Morgan's face. She was surprised at how the 'urge' had hit her again so soon after her last hunt. This was unusual for her.

Despite Jane's ceaseless craving for human flesh, the 'urge'—that intense state of passion that pushed her over the edge into actually tracking down a fellow human being and relieving them of those parts of their body that she fancied—only came on her three or four times a year. This was one reason Jane knew she wasn't insane: it wasn't like she was a salivating savage.

True, I do keep a lot of meat in my basement, but I know where to draw the line. Stocking up four times a year is normal enough. Almost as regular as the seasons.

She paused at the north Eureka Street corner while a pickup truck turned in off Stafford, nodding her head to the pounding rhythms of Slain Jane's *Zombie Takeunder:*

"It's about damn time that we went to bed,
Tomorrow morning we'll all wake up dead,
Or maybe I'll die tonight instead,
Zombies in the queendom of the loving dead . . ."

Alright, yes, the urge isn't actually seasonal. I never seem to feel like hunting in springtime. And sometimes, like two years ago, it's on me almost all the time and it's all I can do not to take a knife out onto the sidewalk and begin slashing at everyone I meet. But I do control it. I never go overboard.

Two years ago *had* been particularly horrible. But horrible in a nice way. She'd hunted ten times that year. The complications had been incredible—weather, logistics, different surgical procedures to master—a pileup of obstacles in her way, but she'd not once failed in her quest to secure the hot human flesh that had caught her attention.

And that WITHOUT KILLING ANYONE either. (To Jane's mind, killing someone for their meat was entirely wrong.)

That year had confirmed to Jane that yes, she really was a genius. She'd harvested so much meat and organs from people that she'd needed to invest in a new freezer to store it all in. Thank heavens for her hidden basement. No one was getting down there that she didn't permit.

The pickup truck passed and she crossed the road, pulling her coat tightly about her to keep out the cold. Her headphones fed her brain music:

"Feeding on hot brains.

Zombie see, zombie do,
Zombie too must poo-poo.
We're all the same,
Rotting and insane,
After the biochemical rain . . ."

CHAPTER 9

Jane & Scott

"Darling, you're so hot, you make the sun jealous."

Jane smiled back at Scott, delighted at the compliment.

Every woman likes to feel appreciated. Despite her IQ of 189, Jane was human, after all. Attractive women need to be told they are attractive all the time; something plain women never expect.

Jane and Scott were having dinner together at his house.

Scott Hamilton. Not exactly the love of Jane's life, but not far off either.

Scott worked at The Bay State Savings Bank and was a widower. He was short, with black hair and gray eyes, middle-aged, and very skinny. A bag of bones with a little paunch.

One thing Jane really liked about Scott was that ever since they'd begun dating ten months ago she hardly ever felt any urge to eat part of him. From a cannibal gourmet point of view, Scott Hamilton was too stringy. He was ridiculously unappealing. Unappetizing in the extreme. Which kept him safe.

Other than for her clandestine activities, Jane was a normal woman with normal relationship expectations and no sexual hang-ups.

A woman needed a man and she had Scott. She liked him, but didn't dare love him. Love was dangerous. Love made you trust people. It made you start to share secrets with them. It put you in their power. It made you their willing slave. Love gave them the ability to hurt you when you least expected it.

So she enjoyed Scott's affection and fucked him regularly. She parted her legs for his erection, came in his arms, and slept in his bed.

But, for obvious reasons, she insisted on living apart from him. She didn't merely value her privacy; it was essential that she lived alone. He could visit her and sleep over as often as he liked, but she wasn't moving in with him. So far too, she'd managed to come up with all sorts of ingenious reasons to not give him a set of keys to her house.

Scott thought she was just paranoid. He'd given her a set of his home keys and let it go.

Jane had high hopes for their shared future. Scott had let her know in more ways than one that he wanted to marry her. He just hadn't gotten down on his knees and presented the diamond ring yet. She was waiting for him to do so. Of course, she'd say yes. She wanted to be married and have a child or two.

She wasn't exactly sure how she'd juggle motherhood, career, and cannibalism (what if she woke up one day with the desire to eat her baby?), but she was certain that given time, she'd figure it out.

All in all, the future looked bright.

Another point in Scott's favor was that he had atrocious taste buds. He couldn't discern a thing. He could hardly tell the difference between meat and chicken. Take tonight, for instance. They were having stewed 'Calf-muscle of Rob Francis' for dinner. But Jane had told Scott that it was specially cured pork, and he believed her. And this wasn't because she'd brought all the meat over from her place. No, he was always like that. Not having the slightest interest in cooking, he ate whatever she fed him with no questions asked. She didn't really blame him though: since his wife's untimely death, most of what he'd been eating had been junk food. Men.

She felt blessed. In her experience, it was really hard to find a man who didn't give a shit what he ate. Jane was very pleased she'd finally found one.

***

Jane liked watching Scott eat. He had very nice table manners, very precise and controlled. He never ate in a hurry.

She, on the other hand, was a very emotional eater, stuffing her mouth or not as the feeling took her. Tonight, for instance, she was in 'slow mode,' intent on tasting every morsel she fed herself, chewing each bite to its limits, hell-bent on extracting the utmost amount of its flavor with her molars before finally permitting the relentlessly pulverized food to visit her stomach.

"So, honey, did anything interesting happen at work today?" Scott asked her between bites of meat.

She shrugged back. "Tony got sacked."

His eyes widened in surprise. "Tony Marler?" Scott knew the tall, anorexic-looking young man. "What'd he do?"

"Drugs."

"Drugs? What? He was shooting up in the toilets?"

Jane didn't really feel like elaborating, but it made a good story. "Well, no one actually caught him doing anything, but recently he'd become paranoid. For the last fortnight he's been claiming to see a monster in the toilets—the *men's* toilets, I mean."

Scott had been forking up some vegetables. He paused and stared at Jane enquiringly. "A monster?"

She shrugged again. "A weird shadow, more like. Said it looked like a giant rabbit. Tony said he'd be in the guys' restroom all alone and he could practically hear it breathing behind him. Nothing reflected in the mirrors, but that huge shadow would suddenly flicker over him. But once he turned around, there was nothing there. Or he'd be outside alone in the corridor and he'd sense it following him; but once again there'd be nothing there when he turned around to look."

"And it was just him? No one else saw it?"

She scowled at Scott. "Hey, don't you start! You sound like you believe him."

Scott shook his head and scratched his neatly trimmed beard. "Of course, I don't believe him. I'm just bemused, is all. It's a weird story." His eyes narrowed. "Well you did say the kid was on drugs."

Jane nodded. She forked some meat into her mouth and chewed it thoroughly before continuing: "Sure he was. Everyone except management knew he was using. Coke and uppers, I think. No one told on him 'cos we all liked him so much. But once he began this new freak-out of his, it became obvious to the bosses too. So, long story short, this afternoon Mr. Ackerman calls Tony into his office and cans him. Couldn't be helped—by this morning, Tony is claiming he can *smell* the giant rabbit; he'd gone to pee and dashed out with his fly open, saying it was in there trying to eat him. So . . . we got a new boy on our shift now—Andrew Sanderson. He's this real serious, mongoloid-looking kid who seems like he kisses management ass for a living. He's always, 'Yes, Mr. Ackerman . . . No, Mr. Ackerman . . . Of course, Mr. Ackerman,' on everything imaginable."

Scott laughed at her description of the new employee. Then he said. "It does seem weird though, doesn't it?"

"What does? Andrew Sanderson's penchant for ass-kissing?"

"No, not that. I mean what Tony claimed he saw. A shapeless monstrosity or shifting colors would be understandable for a guy on drugs. But a giant rabbit, of all things? And over and over again?"

Jane made a show of rolling her eyes. "Oh, just forget it, darling. You're making me regret telling you about it. I for one am sad that Tony's no longer employed at Cashstretch. I'm however delighted not to have to keep hearing about his goddamn giant bunny." She overemphasized an honest-to-God shudder. "That story of his was giving me the creeps. I'd even started doing all my peeing at home before going to work just so I wouldn't need to visit the restroom."

"Honey, I'm just curious."

"Be curious about something else. Scotty, no more comments on the drug addict who got fired. Don't ruin our meal. It took me ages to get this just right. And that after first searching everywhere for the right kind of meat."

Scott looked like he wanted to say some more, but she flashed him her most disarming smile and he kept quiet and ate his dinner like a good boy.

***

They finished eating Rob's leg muscle, washed it down with white wine, and then retired to watch TV in Scott's bedroom.

After a while their emotions spilled over and they made love. They peeled off each other's clothes and lay down in the '69' position.

***

The only time Jane ever got cannibal urges towards her boyfriend was when they made love. Scott Hamilton had a very handsome penis. Jane thought it looked delicious. She often fantasized about smoking the organ and making a sausage out of it. Fellatio was always scary for her because she had to restrain her desires to bite deeply into Scott's erection. Possibly bite it off even. Jane had to constantly remind herself that the penis in her mouth only *felt* like a wiener—it wasn't actually one.

But once they'd both had their orgasms and his manhood had shrunk again, the feeding urge always left her. Then Scott's penis looked as unappealing as the rest of him.

So Scott was very safe with Jane.

***

Oh, what a glorious manhood, Jane thought dreamily, later, when Scott was thrusting into her from behind as they lay like a pair of spoons. *So fat, so hard. Going so deep into the depths of my womanhood. So sweetly penetrating.*

Jane was very passionate. At times, during orgasm she felt like she'd faint away and never revive again.

All in all, it was a good night.

CHAPTER 10

The Urban Legend Investigation People

That same Saturday evening, the TULIP meeting held in Ghost's studio apartment.

'TULIP' stood for 'The Urban Legend Investigation People.'

Out of curiosity, boredom, and in Ghost's case, the simple need to belong to some kind of meaningful organization, those individuals currently assembled in her apartment (and a few others across the state of Massachusetts) had dedicated their free time to separating fact from fiction. To finding out the truth, no matter how weird it was.

It didn't matter if it was ghosts or grave-robbing ghouls, monsters or rumors of alien invasions, TULIP had it covered. Or tried to.

Ghost relaxed in her work chair with her back to her computers. Her visitors had made themselves comfortable wherever they liked. Ninja and Miss Media were on the couch. Playboy was sitting on the floor beside the stereo, with his back against the wall. Avatar and Warrior were both seated on Ghost's bed.

Ghost considered their different clothing styles. To herself, a knowledgeable observer, each individual's clothes provided a neat summary of who they were: Herself, in pink T-shirt and cutoff jeans; Miss Media, in a beige pantsuit (and with her long blonde hair messed up by the wind during the drive over from work in her convertible); Warrior, as always dressed entirely in black leather; Avatar wearing a trench coat he'd refused to take off since arriving (he had removed his hat); Playboy dressed in a navy-blue Gucci pullover and brown Christian Dior slacks; and finally, Ninja, who wore one of the biggest red short-sleeved shirts Ghost had ever seen, and a correspondingly huge pair of pants.

***

Ninja, Miss Media, Avatar . . . ? Those weren't their real names, just how they viewed themselves or how the others viewed them.

Ninja was the brains of the organization, an obese man in his mid-thirties with intense piercing eyes. He'd set up TULIP with his cousin Playboy. Like Ghost, Ninja worked online. He was a hacker who handled major industrial espionage. He sometimes worked for the government too. There was seemingly no level of digital security impossible for Ninja to breach, no digital fortress he couldn't invade. The only way he couldn't find out a thing was if that information wasn't on a computer connected to the internet.

Miss Media was a slender blonde with an elfin face. She was a genius. In 'real life' she worked at Boston City Hall. She was called 'Miss Media' because she operated all of TULIP's surveillance equipment. If an ant moved, she'd get it on record. She could bug an entire apartment block and none of its occupants would be any the wiser.

Playboy could have been *The Bachelor*. He was tall, muscular, and excruciatingly handsome, with dark hair and laughing eyes. Women flocked to him in droves. He always had a woman on his arm. In 'real life,' he was a rich brat, the heir to a multimillion automobile empire. Playboy was Ninja's cousin and funded most TULIP investigations. As with everything else in life, the money had to come from somewhere.

Avatar was tall too, but spindly. He looked as sneaky as his name suggested—like a chameleon. He was a con artist, was willing to sell you Logan Airport if you were dumb enough to want it. Or his old crippled mother, if you didn't mind taking her wheelchair and colostomy bag too. But he was an expert in opening locks and could wriggle into (and out of) just about anywhere.

And finally, Warrior. Warrior was a small man who could apparently handle every single weapon in existence. Didn't matter what it was, or if it was old or modern, Warrior had it covered. He also had black belts in Karate, Judo, and several obscure martial arts the others had never heard off. Sometimes the impossible things TULIP hunted (or the people hiding and protecting those things) could be deadly. Warrior ensured that they all got out alive after Avatar had gotten them 'in' and Miss Media had recorded anything there was to see.

They lived in different Massachusetts towns: Playboy and Miss Media resided in Boston, Ninja and Ghost in Worcester (which was central to them and easiest for everyone to drive to). Avatar lived in Springfield and Warrior in Agawam.

***

TULIP's motto was simple: 'Hide all you like; we'll find out for real.'

***

The first order of business at this evening's meeting was reviewing their most recent investigation. That had been a search for the Rat King, a supposed mutant rumored to live in a series of tunnels deep in the bowels of Honwee Mountain (near the state's western border), and which could direct rodents to do its deadly and murderous bidding.

"Alright," Ninja said after they'd been conferring for about an hour, "I'd say that about concludes this debriefing." He gestured with his cold beer to the blonde woman seated beside him on the coach. "You got anything to add, Media?"

Since she kept better records than anyone else, Miss Media also functioned as club secretary. "Nah, everything's complete. As expected, the videos on tulipinvestigates.com are getting some heavy views, but of course, it's like always: people are so inundated with fake news and shit on YouTube, they don't know what to believe anymore." She laughed. "One troll's comment was to ask what film studio did the special effects for us." She waited for everyone's laughter to subside before adding: "I'm not kidding you guys—the guy's an independent filmmaker; he wants to hire them for his next horror flick."

"Sometimes I wonder why we do this," Avatar said, running fingers through his short brown hair. "We might just as well hire a CGI wizard to create some monsters for us. He'd have done a great Rat King."

Ninja laughed at that.

"We do it for the thrill of knowing?" Ghost pointed out. "Dude, you know, like, to actually know *for sure* about things like that? We do it 'cos . . . someone has to?" She'd had some wine and felt slightly feisty. She wasn't in the mood for Avatar's negativity.

Avatar nodded. "Yeah, yeah, so we say." Then seeing her expression turn dour, he added, "No, I'm not baiting you, spooky lady. It's just how the public always seems to prefer fake news over the truth that riles me up."

Playboy dragged on the joint he was smoking, then said, "Well, guys, be that as it may, I'm with the pretty Ghost on this: we now know the truth about the Rat King—we've actually *seen* him. We've seen what he can do." He nodded forward. "Warrior has even felt his power."

Warrior scowled back at him. "You lot still haven't thanked me for pulling your asses out of that pit of rats." He waved his bandaged right arm at Playboy. "Next time, rich guy, I'm gonna leave ya to get your fair share of the bites . . . and the accompanying rabies shots." He looked around. "Same goes for all of you—any more wisecracks tonight and next time you'll be rescuing your own asses."

Everyone restrained their intense desire to laugh . . .

***

Ghost didn't even feel like laughing. She still shuddered to think of what they'd found down there in those catacomb-like tunnels inside Honwee Mountain: that hideously deformed furry thing that was more animal than human, sitting on a hill of wet human bones, with its squeaky voice that had dispatched seemingly a thousand rats at them. Some of the rats had been as deformed as their mutant ruler, with extra legs and heads.

The rats had streamed out of pits in the tunnel floor, poured from holes in its walls, and also dropped en masse from cracks in its ceiling. It had only been Warrior's quick thinking, in pouring gasoline on the walls and floor and igniting it, that had saved them. And even then, some of the crazed and hungry rodents had leapt through the 'U' of fire in their path, seeking the human prey the Rat King was siccing them on. The rats burst into flame in midair but came on regardless, the intent to kill glowing in their little black eyes. Warrior had made a second wall of fire, and some of them had leapt through that one also.

Certain she was about dying right there and then, Ghost had turned and fled, as had the others. It was Warrior who'd faced down those rats which had made it past the obstruction of fire.

All the TULIP members had made it out alive, though with bruises and torn clothes. Ninja had been so exhausted by their flight that he'd instantly collapsed on the grass by the cave entrance and begun gasping like he was asthmatic.

Then, their hearts in their mouths, they'd all waited for Warrior. None of them had dared reenter the cave to go look for him. When Warrior finally emerged from the underground tunnels, his entire right forearm dripped with blood from rat bites.

So Warrior had saved them all. Otherwise they'd all be gnawed skeletons now, somewhere in the west of the state, with a thing that looked like a hairless baboon defecating on their bones as it added them to its hideous collection.

***

Warrior was still scowling at everyone. The reason no one was saying anything now was for the same reason Ghost had fallen silent: everyone was remembering the Rat King. It wasn't a nice memory at all. Made you wonder why you did it, but for a different reason than Avatar had raised—it made you wonder if you were suicidal.

Miss Media recovered first. She addressed Warrior in a soft, mocking voice: "Darling, I thought you did it for the thrill of danger?"

He grinned a cobra's grin. "Alright, Media, next time you're gonna get the shit bit out of you. And I hope we're hunting giant gators then."

Miss Media turned pale for a moment. Of course he didn't mean that. But what if he did? "Aw c'mon, man, I'm just fooling with you. You know we're tighter than assholes and I worship the very arm you let the rats gnaw on my behalf. Can't you take a joke?"

"Nope."

"Please, baby?"

He smiled coldly. "Media, just pray that what Ninja's brought us all here for tonight is something sweet and safe. Or else, you're monster food, baby."

She pouted.

Why the hell am I even with these guys? Ghost wondered as she watched the interplay between the pair. *Just to be a token female in some boy's club?*

But she knew that wasn't true. There were other women in TULIP, not just Miss Media. And though she'd mainly joined TULIP because the idea of investigating urban legends sounded fun, Ghost had to agree with Miss Media's initial retort to Warrior: the thrill of danger played a huge part in keeping her from growing bored with their 'truth club' and quitting it.

Fleeing the Rat King's ravenous minions had been the scariest experience of Ghost's life, but the adrenalin rush of it? Damn, that had been unbeatable. Ghost had never felt like that before: her heart pumping as if it would blow a hole in her chest, her every sense more alive than during orgasm, her whole body alert to the danger; knowing in her soul that only a few inches or motions—maybe just a single stumble—separated her from horrible scurrying hungry death.

And afterwards, once they'd all made it back to Ninja's place and were relaxing, she'd felt reborn, purified from her old self.

Ninja was speaking again. "You know, Media, if I were you I'd really plead with Warrior in private"—he winked salaciously at her—"after this. 'Cos you know you don't wanna be left behind on this next investigation I'm about proposing."

She looked narrowly at him. "Oh, Warrior and I are as tight as a pair of catwalk butt-cheeks. The man was just joking."

Warrior laughed coldly. "I might not be."

Miss Media froze for a moment, then scowled at him. "Stop it, will you! You're giving me the damn heebie-jeebies."

He shrugged.

"So what's this new search you've got planned for us all?" Ghost asked.

A broad smile on his face, Ninja announced, "I think it's time that TULIP investigates the legend of Insane Jane."

"Who's that?" Ghost immediately enquired.

"She's supposedly a cannibal," Playboy replied her from his spot on the floor.

Ghost was unimpressed. "*Another* cannibal? That's ordinary, man. We hear enough creepy tales of inbred rednecks waylaying lost travelers and having them for dinner. But not up here in Massachusetts. Down in West Virginia in the Appalachian mountains, maybe. I thought TULIP was supposed to be sticking to weirdness native to our state."

Playboy shook his head. "Not this lady, Ghost. This one ain't just another routine anthropophagus." He stubbed out his joint, then got up to pace the floor, beaming his handsomest smile at them all. "What makes this lady Jane different is that she's an *urban* cannibal." He gestured with a brawny hand. "And she's never been caught, not even on film. No one knows who she is. Her entire existence is just a nasty rumor."

While Ghost pondered on that and scratched an itch on her thigh, Avatar asked: "So if she's never been filmed, how do we know she exists?"

"Oh, there's a frigging shitload of evidence," Miss Media replied. "Ninja and I have checked out all the available data and found it to be completely legit." She nodded at Playboy to go on.

Playboy continued: "See, the unique thing about Insane Jane—and I think how she's been able to operate for so long—is, Jane doesn't kill people to eat them. No, she's smarter than that."

Ghost looked perplexed. "No? So how does she get her meat then? She's a ghoul? She visits morgues or unearths the recently buried?"

Playboy laughed and shook his head. "No. Nothing at all like that. According to the legend, Insane Jane visits her victims at home and cuts off those portions of their bodies that she wants to eat. She drugs the person—man or woman—removes whatever flesh she wants from them, and then, in serious cases, leaves them a cellphone to call for an ambulance."

Ghost shivered. "For real?"

As if for effect, Miss Media uncrossed then re-crossed her legs. Then she nodded. "For real, baby. This is a true urban nightmare we're talking about here. Imagine waking up at three a.m. one morning and finding that all the meat on your thighs is gone, that there's nothing between your hips and knees except bare stripped bones."

"What?" Avatar gasped. "Who could be so sick in the head as to do that?"

Playboy smirked at him. "Dude, the lady ain't called *Insane* Jane for no reason."

"Ugh," Warrior said. "Now that's what I call crazy for real." He picked his can of beer up off the rug, took a long pull from it, then added, "Guys, I gotta tell ya, I already friggin' *love* this new investigation."

"Man, we haven't voted on it yet," Ghost said, then shivered again. All of a sudden she had a queasy feeling in the pit of her stomach. She felt troubled. She sensed that this investigation might backfire on them all in a really bad way. "And I'm telling you guys straight off that my vote is 'No.' I want nothing to do with this 'Insane Jane' woman."

Warrior laughed coldly. "You scared, spooky?"

"Damn right, I'm frigging scared." She turned away from Warrior and stared coldly at Ninja. "Hey, man, what the vagina fuck is going on with you and Playboy? How come each of these investigations gets more and more crazy? Why can't we just investigate mundane stuff like alligators in the sewers or corn circles?"

Ninja shrugged his fat shoulders. "That's already been checked out. No, we need to boldly go where no club's ever gone before."

Playboy grinned at Ghost. "Beam us down to Hell, spooky."

"If we're already voting on this," Warrior said, "my vote's a definite *hell yeah!*"

"Hell no!" Ghost insisted. "I don't think you guys get the point here."

Miss Media yawned, revealing her fillings. "Which is, darling?"

"What if this crazy woman starts stalking *us?*" She shuddered. "C'mon, you guys, be reasonable. I, for one, don't wanna wake up someday to find out half of my legs are gone."

"Yeah," Miss Media agreed. "You've got great legs. Be a shame to wake up at dawn and find them missing."

Ghost gave her the finger.

"Hey, let up, you two." Ninja adjusted his ponderous bulk on the couch. "And, Ghost, you're already outvoted. Media, Playboy and myself are already for doing this, and I can see that Warrior is too—"

"Dang straight I is—if you'll forgive me speaking Texan." He'd pulled out a pistol and was sighting along its barrel towards Ghost, which only made her feel worse.

Playboy had meanwhile taken a seat on the windowsill. Beyond him, the day was darkening. It was 8 p.m. now. Ghost began hoping they'd finish this discussion on time so she could attend her Safe Word sex meeting. (That would at least relax her.) But, she already doubted such would be the case. A new investigation always brought a lot of talk along with it.

Ninja went on: "—Which leaves just Avatar here left to vote on it. According to club rules, anyone who isn't at a meeting agrees with whatever decision the attendees take." He looked at Avatar. "Dude, you're already in this whatever you say. We got four to two on you. But just for the record, what do you say?"

Avatar looked nervous. But then, he always looked nervous. "I'm with Ghost on this. But like you just pointed out, my vote's just for the record anyway. So, alright, we're doing this, but I intensely dislike it." His thin face creased up into a frown. "Tell us: what do we know about this woman?"

"Duh? She eats people?" Ghost growled, rolling her eyes. "Have you been asleep all this while?"

He waved her off. "I mean, aside from that?"

Ghost stared pointedly at Ninja. "Yes, do enlighten us, o mighty leader."

He shrugged. "It's like everything else we research into: first of all, Insane Jane may or may not exist, but if she does—"

"Hey, wait just a sec," Ghost interrupted him. "Her name—Jane. How does a figment of one's imagination have a definite name for reference?"

Miss Media told her, "It's *not* specific. She's called that 'cos no one's certain of her real name. Jane Doe, you know? Insane Jane Doe?"

"Oh." Ghost nodded at Ninja. "Continue with what you were saying, man."

"Yeah," Ninja confirmed, "the woman's name may not even be Jane at all. It could be Maureen, or Nina, or Caroline—"

"Or Hansel's sister Gretel, or the goddamn witch who wants to roast them both," Warrior broke in on him. "Alright, we get it. Get on with it. I'm impatient to start hunting this wonderful woman."

"I would if you'd all stop interrupting me." Ninja looked around the room. He waited until everyone had nodded their agreement to keep quiet back at him, before going on: "Okay, I'll cut right to the damn chase. What we do know about our Jane is that she's a—"

Ghost put her hand up. "Sorry to interrupt again, man. Last time ever, but I really got a question." She made an apologetic face. "Please?"

"Alright. What is it?"

"How do we know it's a woman? Couldn't it be a guy?"

"Very unlikely. A few victims woke up during their drastic 'surgery'—let's call it that—and they had a glimpse of a dark-haired woman in surgical garb doing the unthinkable to them . . . Now, this brings me to a point—Insane Jane has to be a medical professional of some kind. This lady isn't just some backstreet butcher. Each 'operation' of hers is carried out with surgical tools and proper surgical procedure. I mean, no one's died on her yet, and, with exception of the heart and brain, she's removed just about every imaginable organ from her victim's bodies. From the stories, she uses hemostats, tourniquets, ligatures, and even cauterizers to stop blood loss. She's also an expert in the use of anesthetics. Each victim simply fell asleep and woke up missing something. No pain, nothing. Even those victims who woke up while she was cutting them up reported not feeling a damn thing . . . not even the injection that put them back to sleep again."

"So we're looking for a psycho medico," Ghost said before remembering she was supposed to be keeping quiet. "How many victims so far?"

"Twenty-seven. All of them here in Massachusetts. Different towns though; with no logical connect between 'em so far that Media, Playboy and I can determine. She may have more victims outside our state, but no one knows for sure."

"That's an extraordinary run of luck," Warrior commented. "She'd be a hit in Las Vegas. What do the cops know about her?"

"Nothing at all," Playboy replied him. "Ninja's hacked into the State Police databases. Even the FBI know next to nothing."

Ghost gave Playboy a weird look. "Nothing?"

He nodded back, then ran a hand over his dark hair. She thought he too looked spooked by this thing he'd helped set in motion. And that after they'd both seen the Rat King?

This case just gets more 'don't fucking touch' by the minute. But of course, we're gonna touch it. 'Cos that's what we do—charge in where angels fear to tread.

"Yeah, girl, nothing at all," Playboy finally replied, then looked away from her and out of the window, where it was full night now. "That's why this goddamned caper I let my cousin talk me into is so dangerous."

"No, that's why it's so fucking exciting," Warrior corrected him, flapping the edges of his black jacket like they were crow wings. "We do it for the danger, for the thrill of feeling alive . . . of feeling the blood coursing through our veins, and our hearts pumping blood like never before."

"Speak for yourself, dude," Avatar said. "I do it 'cos occasionally we meet pretty women who need saving and I'm looking to get laid. And, as far as this case goes? Personally, I can already feel my balls playing tag with my kidneys."

Warrior laughed. "Nah, that's just your lunch disagreeing with you. Expect some gas at your ass shortly." He pulled out his gun again and examined it from different angles.

Miss Media returned their discussion to its previous course: "Lady and gentlemen, here's why Insane Jane seems to be a myth—she apparently has no fingerprints."

"How the vagina fuck is that possible?" Ghost asked.

Miss Media tossed back her blonde hair with a flick of her head. "Dunno. According to those police reports Ninja hacked for us, their investigation—it's ongoing but permanently stalled for lack of evidence—shows that at each crime scene, the forensics guys can't find nada to pinpoint who's responsible. No DNA traces, no hair strands, no fabric or bodily fluids; nothing. It's almost like a ghost did it." She flung Ghost an apologetic glance. "I don't mean you, darling—the supernatural kind of spook."

"It would be real nice if this lady doesn't exist," Ninja said. "But from what we've dug up so far, it's eight to two that she does." He shifted his huge bulk on the couch, sipped some beer, and grinned a broad, fat grin at the others. "Guys, view it this way: we owe it to the public to find this crazy lady and put a halt to her activities."

Ghost nodded. "Alright, alright, all-vagina-fucking-right. When you put it like that I gotta agree with you—we *do* need to stop this woman." Using her right index finger, she drew a rough shape of the state of Massachusetts in the air. "But where do we start looking?"

"Yeah," Avatar seconded. "What have you mentally deficient guys who are dragging us off to hunt this evil cannibalistic witch so far discovered about her whereabouts?"

"We think she lives here in Worcester," Miss Media said simply. She grinned at Ghost. "May even be one of your closest friends or neighbors."

"What the vagina fuck?" Ghost felt horrified. She imagined herself waking up on a cold autumn morning with all the flesh and skin on both of her arms missing, with just useless pale bones sticking out from each shoulder and running down to stripped skeletal fingers that seemed made of white chalk. She gaped at Miss Media. "She's here in town?"

Ninja grinned broadly at Ghost's discomfort. "The evidence suggests as much. So, baby, it's in both of our best interests to find her and halt her activities as soon as possible."

CHAPTER 11

Scott, Caitlin & Jane . . . Next Weekend

"You know, honey, I still find it hard to get my mind around how many medical textbooks you own."

It was a comment that Scott Hamilton had made often in the ten months he'd been dating Jane Winters.

Now, staring at the rows of books that filled the larger of Jane's two living room bookshelves, Scott repeated it.

"What was that, darling?" Jane called from the kitchen. She was in there fixing dinner, along with Scott's daughter Caitlin who was in town from Boston.

"I'm just appreciating how well-read you are," he called back. "A whole lotta medical books you got here."

Jane, dressed in a white smock and blue apron, and looking every inch the busy housewife, leaned out of the kitchen for a moment. "Yeah, they really are many, aren't they?"

Scott ran his fingers over a thick hardback textbook on the coffee table. It was opened up to a glossy image of a dissected female face. It was a horrible image, he felt, seeing a person's head all opened up like that. "You sure do take this stuff seriously, honey."

"I really do want to attend medical school someday. I just hope I'm not leaving things too late."

Scott smiled nicely. "Oh, I don't think you are, honey. I'm sure the AMA can use one more member. But still"—his gaze left her for a moment and moved right, to the corner of the living room where she had a complete plastic human skeleton set up—"Still, don't you think you're overdoing things just a little bit? I mean, this is the *third* skeleton you've bought. Earlier, when we arrived, Caitlin thought you were gearing up for Halloween. And . . . and you've got more medical books in this house than my doctor has in his office."

She laughed, a pleasant musical tinkle, that, had Scott Hamilton been more discerning and not so head-over-heels in love with her, he'd have considered a little psychotic. "It's my obsession, Scotty. I can have just one, can't I?"

He rubbed his forehead. "Yeah, of course you can. But I don't want you putting yourself in an asylum."

Her face turned serious; almost as if she was about getting angry with him. "Oh? How d'you mean? You're not suggesting that I'm crazy to have all these books, are you?"

He shook his head. "Not at all. Even a blind shrink can see you're saner than I am. I'm just worried for your mental health if you keep studying so hard before you've even been accepted into med school, what with your working so hard at Cashstretch too. Remember, you ain't getting any younger, lady."

Her tension visibly left her. Her face relaxed. She laughed again. "You're mixing things up, sweetheart. You're the middle-aged one, not me. And I'll have you know that I once scored very high on an IQ test, though I don't remember what it was about now . . . Oh shit, Caitlin, what are you doing to my soup?"

She turned away from him and ducked back into the kitchen. Scott could hear she and his daughter having a mumbled conversation which, the kitchen disaster having apparently been averted, promptly dissolved into loud feminine giggles.

Well, at least they're getting along, he thought. That had been his primary worry when Caitlin had asked to meet "that pretty lady you've been hiding from me": that as potential step-relatives often did, they'd hate each other on sight and would then proceed to make his life unbearable with complaints about each other.

But thankfully, that didn't seem to be the case here. He was very relieved. *One less heart attack to fear then.*

Scott took one more look at Jane's opened medical textbook. Then he went to sit down and sip the glass of wine she'd earlier poured him.

CHAPTER 12

Caitlin

Caitlin Hamilton didn't know what to make of her father's new girlfriend. On the surface, Jane Winters seemed perfect, exactly what she'd wanted for her father since her mother's death. A woman to make him happy again.

(Not like that other Jane whom her father had dated several years back. Caitlin hadn't been able to stand the woman. She'd been delighted when Jane Summers had finally dissolved the relationship and vanished from their lives.)

But, it was Jane's very perfection which worried Caitlin. Jane seemed too good to be true. And usually when people seemed that way, that's what they were: too good to be true.

Following Jane out of the kitchen with a tray of steaming venison soup, Caitlin decided to give her the benefit of the doubt.

Raven-haired herself, with her hair cut in severe bangs for that 'executive-in-waiting' look, Caitlin felt more than a twinge of envy while observing Jane's long red hair. The hair spilled halfway down Jane's back and looked like fire, like phoenix flames falling from her head. The older woman's green eyes also sparked envy in Caitlin, whose own light-colored eyes never really stood out.

Maybe I'm just jealous. She's attractive, funny, and genuinely seems to care about dad. What more do I want? Or is it that I think she's too young for him? Would I feel more comfortable seeing him with a woman closer his own age? Do I think she's going to be in competition with me for dad's affection?

Caitlin indeed felt she had a better view of the young redhead than her father did. For one thing, she was just twenty-four, almost Jane's own age of twenty-eight (one of the first details she'd wormed out of Scott once she'd heard him calling someone 'honey' on the phone). And secondly, she wasn't love-smitten like her father was. The way he'd been fawning over Jane Winters since they'd arrived here seemed more like a movie romance than real life.

But, there was just something about this perfect woman that Caitlin sensed was 'off.' And yet, she couldn't be sure:

Am I just scared that he's getting more of a second daughter than a wife? And that I'm gonna wind up with a bossy 'older sister?' Oh, he hasn't yet told me of any marriage plans, but that's the way it goes, isn't it? Dating leads to sex, or sex leads to dating, which leads to engagements and weddings and honeymoons and new brothers and sisters.

They ate. And it was here that Caitlin got her first true inkling of Miss Perfect Winters being somewhat less than perfect: Jane ate like a savage. She ate 'viciously,' as if at loggerheads with the food. She spooned her soup into her mouth at a ferocious pace, forked up her vegetables like she was a bulldozer clearing a bomb site, and chewed like a car compactor pulverizing a Corvette. She ate as if she'd been starving forever. Not messily, but intently, with her eyes bulging just a little bit.

That's it!—she eats like an animal. A pretty animal, but nonetheless something from a jungle somewhere. She looks very ugly while eating, but a very attractive sort of ugly. No wonder dad's besotted with her.

This last was evident. Scott seemed oblivious to everything Caitlin was noticing. He beamed at Jane with almost paternal indulgence as she ate, taking pleasure in everything she did.

Wow, Caitlin thought. *I really wish I could find a guy to love me like this!*

While eating her own dinner, Caitlin found it hard to take her eyes off their redhead hostess. Jane's ingenuous feeding behavior was bewitching to behold.

On the food front? This soup they were having tasted a little strange to Caitlin. While they'd been preparing it, Jane had explained that the meats they were using were a mixture of venison and rabbit. Caitlin, however, felt the soup also had a high pork content. It was delicious though. Jane was a very good cook.

Another plus in her favor where dad's concerned. I really should be happy for him that he's found her. Why then do I feel . . . ?

She didn't know what she felt. Uneasy? Conflicted, maybe.

Jane was speaking to her: "Aren't you enjoying the food, Caitlin? You seem a little preoccupied."

"No, it's fine, honest. Delicious. It's just work troubles that never let one go, no matter where one goes."

Jane laughed. "Tell me about it. Scotty says you work for an ad agency. That has to be really exciting."

Caitlin managed a laugh and shook her head. "Only on primetime TV, I'm afraid. In the real world, it's just one boring day after another. You'd think writing copy would inspire you, right? But after ten or so ad campaigns for products you neither use nor care about, it's just the same as anything else." She grinned. "It pays good though."

Scott chipped in: "Hey, honeybunch, tell Janie about the vanished executive. What was her name again?"

Jane stared at Scott with interest, then turned to Caitlin. "Vanished executive? What's he talking about?"

Caitlin swallowed a mouthful of soup and shrugged. "Oh, dad, you mean Ms. Schreiber." She shrugged again, at Jane this time. "Well, see, it's a really creepy tale. We had this one executive at our office— Jessica Schreiber—I mean, a real high-powered chick, super-hard worker and all . . . a really nice lady, but a complete workaholic . . . you know, the sort that finds excuses to sleep in the office, and not 'cos the boss wants to examine their underwear?"

Caitlin relaxed as she warmed to her tale. "Well, so, last year, during an ad presentation, Ms. Schreiber just ups and collapses during the meeting."

"Collapses?"

Caitlin nodded, then sipped some white wine. "Yeah, she slumps to the floor, out cold—we had to rush her to hospital. I was there, saw it happen. Turns out that she's completely exhausted. Wiped out by her endless working without rest. She'd not taken a vacation for years. So . . . our bosses all send her off to Raynham. They don't want to see her for six months, they say, or else . . . So then, Ms. Schreiber, along with two of her best friends, travels to Raynham for her vacation. And then all three of them vanish . . . simply vanish into thin air."

"How?"

"No one knows. It just happens. Apparently they stayed in this nice house on some kind of private estate for about a week, and then each of them left for different locations—they each checked into hotels in different parts of the country, and that was the last anyone ever saw of the three of them."

Jane was gaping at her. "For real?"

"Yeah, seriously. I think the other two women were named Lucy and Rebecca. Yes, Rebecca. There was a huge search, because Rebecca was a heiress and her rich family made all kinds of attempts to locate her—they hired three different firms of private investigators, I think. But all to no avail. Not a trace of the three of them was found. And no one's heard from any of them till this moment."

"That is creepy," Jane said. "To think that someone could just vanish like that."

Caitlin nodded. "Yeah, creepy as hell. Like an alien abduction thing."

Scott said, "Alien abduction my ass. Personally, honeybunch, I think a serial killer got the three of them." He shook his head. "Poor women."

Caitlin asked, "Jane, where's the ladies' room? I think my breakfast just caught up with my lunch and both of them are having an argument with my dinner."

Jane pushed her own chair back and stood up. "Come, I'll show you. I need to have a little tinkle myself."

Caitlin got up and followed her.

"I find it really scary that something like that can happen to people in this modern day and age," Jane said as she led her guest from the dining room. "I mean, three women just vanishing like that."

"Are you telling me? And she was such a nice woman too. Someone I looked up to as a role model. I shudder each time I think of how I'll never see her again."

"I know what you mean. It's like no one's safe nowadays. No one at all. Just imagine . . ."

CHAPTER 13

Father & Daughter

Later, as Scott drove them home in his silver Ford Fusion, he asked Caitlin: "So . . . ?"

Caitlin at first pretended not to understand. "So what, daddy?"

"Don't 'daddy' me. So . . . what do you think of Janie?"

"Oh, she's a nice lady. I like her. I really do. I'm just not sure if . . . Hey, I don't think I should be saying this. I don't wanna come between you and your love life or anything."

Scott laughed. "Fat chance of that happening." He sobered a little. "But, please go on. I'm curious as to what you've noticed."

"Hey, you're the one asking. Don't blame me later for whatever I say."

"Yes, honeybunch, you're forgiven beforehand. I promise I won't make you disappear like your boss did."

"And, dad, *please* stop calling me 'honeybunch' in public. It's embarrassing. I'm not fifteen anymore."

Scott reached over to the passenger seat and ruffled Caitlin's hair, which made her squirm. "Sorry, honeybunch." He turned onto Salisbury Street, then slowed when the van in front of them showed its brake lights before it turned onto Rutland Terrace. "Yeah, go on, tell me what you think about Janie."

"You really sure you wanna know?"

He grinned. "I'm a man, I can take it." Then he laughed. "And if I can't, you'll be the first to know 'cos I'll lose control of this car right after my heart attack."

"Okay, you're the one asking. Like I said, she seems wonderful—pretty and clever, a wonderful cook, wonderful hostess—"

"She's wonderful too in other ways that I ain't telling an innocent kid like you about. Speaking of which, how are things going between you and Stu?"

Caitlin shrugged. "So-so. We aren't sure yet if we wanna commit to each other."

"But you've been dating for over a year! Isn't that commitment enough?"

"It should be, but—hey, dad, don't you dare change the topic! We're talking about *your* love life, not mine."

"Sorry. You're right. I'm just perplexed. Here I am trying to get married for the second time, while—like many of your generation—you don't seem to be able to manage even a first matrimony."

She scowled at him in the Ford's dark interior. "Dad, stop it!"

He grinned some more. "Go on . . ."

"Okay . . . well, the way Jane eats, for instance. It's borderline disgusting? Like you go out to a restaurant with her and everyone else is gonna be staring at the two of you?"

"Oh, that ain't her fault. Her aunt starved her as a child; she's never gotten over the experience."

"Starved her?"

"Yeah. She never talks about it much, but apparently her guardians tried to control her by food deprivation. It only stopped when she got into high school and threatened to make a fuss. But still, it's messed her up—she says that each time she sees food now, she's scared it's gonna be taken away from her, so she's got to eat it as fast as possible."

Caitlin mused on that. "Ugh, that's just horrible. But, dad . . . okay, there's also the other strange thing I noticed: why isn't there a single mirror in her house? After using the toilet I noticed there wasn't any in there—you can see the lighter spot on the wall where it was removed from—so I asked her if she had a little one I could borrow, since I'd left my handbag outside in the living room. But she said she didn't have any, none at all in the house." She forced a laugh. "So, Dad, please explain that one to me. Are you dating a vampire or what?"

Scott slowed the car as they reached a turning, then scratched his beard. "She hates mirrors, girl. She's got a massive aversion to them."

"Yeah, I kinda figured as much. But *why* does she hate them?"

"I've no idea, honeybunch. She doesn't seem to know why herself. It seems to also stem from something that happened in her childhood.

Something really ugly. I've urged her to see a shrink about it, but she bluntly refuses to." He paused speaking for a moment, examining the streetlamp-lit road ahead. "You know that because of that, she never wears makeup?"

"I've been wondering how she'd manage to doll herself up for your outside dates if she doesn't have any mirrors at home."

He laughed. "She doesn't. Not that I think I'd ever notice the difference if she did. I'm just delighted to have her. Lipstick or no lipstick."

"She makes you happy, I can see that."

"Oh, yes she does, honeybunch. She really does."

"Stop calling me 'honeybunch!' "

"C'mon, doll, we aren't in public now."

"Don't call me 'doll' either. I'm not Barbie either!"

Her father was clearly very happy, tapping on the steering wheel as he drove like there was music playing in her head. Caitlin lacked the heart to tell him her biggest worry: that Jane Winters was merely putting on an 'I Love You' act to please him. Despite Jane's charm, Caitlin sensed a cold core to her. To her, Jane was a fur coat draped over a refrigerator—delightfully warm on the outside, full of frigidity within. She just hoped the woman her father loved wouldn't wind up breaking his heart. Or worse.

Caitlin worried that Jane's fear of mirrors might be indicative of a personal disgust with herself. Or of repressed suicidal tendencies. If such was the case, Jane could conceivably someday decide to kill herself. And viewing her romance as some sort of deranged one-sided suicide pact, she might kill her lover too.

And why, Caitlin pondered, *why is every second book she's got at home something on advanced surgical procedures? Yeah, yeah, I know she wants to be a doctor someday, but dad's right—she's taking it way too far. She's even got a DVD collection of surgical procedures!*

While Caitlin wrestled with her thoughts, they'd arrived in the Forest Grove neighborhood, were almost home. At the Mormon Church on Chester Street, Scott turned the car left onto Bjorklund Avenue. He lived 300 yards down Bjorklund.

There was something else that Caitlin Hamilton would have liked to tell her father, but she knew if she mentioned it he'd just laugh at her. It was the fact that while she'd been using the toilet at Jane's place, she'd seen something flicker across the toilet walls. A weird shadow of some sort. Weird because, well, the only thing she could liken it to at the time had been a rabbit jumping.

She'd blinked and it was gone. But of course, it had never been there in the first place. Just a trick of the light, which had nonetheless spooked her, even before she'd realized that her hostess didn't have any mirrors in her house.

"Oh, I'm just being childish," she mumbled under her breath. *Maybe I should mention it to dad. No, he'll simply call me 'honeybunch' again and have a really good laugh at my expense. And he's so in love with his Lady Jane that he might mention it to her and then I'll never live it down.*

Instead, Caitlin grinned at her father as he steered the car into their driveway. "Well, one thing's for certain, daddy. You certainly picked a great cook this time."

Scott Hamilton laughed. He parked the silver Ford Fusion, and they went into the house.

CHAPTER 14

Jane, Megan & Karen

A Saturday night.

The Morgan sisters lived on the far east side of Worcester, in a small two-story house on Palisades Street in the Hamilton neighborhood. Jane had already visited here once, two nights ago, to get a good understanding of the building's layout.

Jane always did this while stalking prey: went to their homes and had a look around. It helped her plan her raids better. On that previous visit to the Morgan sister's house, she'd determined that the building had no burglar alarm. Robert Francis's house *had* had one, but she'd successfully disarmed it the night before he'd lost his legs to her. Unknown to her boyfriend Scott, Jane didn't just have books on medicine at home. Down in her basement, she had an entire library of books on burglary, abduction, home security devices and whatnot. Entering a house uninvited was no big deal to her.

It bothered Jane sometimes, how easy she found it to enter people's houses and subdue them. She liked to think that this was simply because she was good at what she did. But she had a recurring sense of a 'helper,' an unseen force assisting her in fulfilling her 'purpose.'

Or else, she'd occasionally pondered, *how is it that I've never once had trouble doing this? Not even once? Locks on doors, chains, alarm systems—none of those have ever posed a problem for me.*

Using one of several sets of skeleton keys she possessed, Jane let herself in via the Morgans' back door. She was dressed entirely in black denim. To avoid possible recognition, she wore both a black wig and black makeup. Her equally black van was parked in the road outside the Morgan home, with black towels draped over its number plates.

Jane silently slipped into the house and put down her two suitcases. These contained everything she'd need.

She shut the door behind her. Carrying two syringes, each containing a carefully mixed combination of sedatives and painkillers, she made her stealthy way up the stairs.

***

On Jane's previous visit to their home, Megan and Karen Morgan had been watching TV together, complete with a bucket of fried chicken between them. The movie had been an old rom-com from the sixties.

This time, however, Jane discovered the two young women making love. Karen was lying naked on the living room couch with her legs spread, her left foot up on top of the couch's back. Her eyes were shut and she was moaning with pleasure. Megan, who still had on a red bra, was sitting beside her. Megan's fingers were deep inside Karen's vagina.

Wow, Jane thought, *sisters really are doing it for themselves.*

She felt disgusted. She wasn't turned on in the least. It wasn't the lesbianism—Jane simply felt that incest was wrong. If you were going to do it, do it outside the family. Incest created low IQ morons.

Though upset at being delayed in accomplishing her objective, Jane settled down to watch the sisters fuck. She sat down in the dark corner behind an armchair.

Megan and Karen were oblivious to her presence. The reason for this was quickly obvious: a half-empty bottle of bourbon on the coffee table. There weren't any glasses—the girls had been drinking directly from the bottle. In the ashtray beside the whiskey bottle, two half-smoked cigarettes trailed pale wisps of smoke upward. As a possible indication of how long Karen and Megan had been making love, both cigarettes had inch-long tails of ash attached to them.

Beyond the two women the TV showed a old ghost flick.

"Give it to me, darling sister," Karen gasped, thrusting her crotch forward and impaling herself on Megan's fingers. "Make me come too!"

Megan repositioned herself. She knelt on the couch, folded Karen's legs up onto her breasts, and began licking her. She had a very long tongue, one that reached out almost to her chin. Jane admired the strokes the tongue made over the younger girl's sex, pink and wet, flesh sweeping over flesh; then *into* her, a pink spade digging deep into the furrow between Karen's blonde ridges of genital fur.

Megan spread the vagina gaping-wide and spat on it. Spat inside it. She opened her younger sister up as wide as a mouth and spat inside her again. Her sputum formed white bubbles against the juicy pink flesh of the orifice. She bent lower and kissed the toothless wet and red lower mouth, then stuck her tongue inside it once more.

Karen gasped. She moaned. She gripped the edges of the couch and squeezed them hard. She dripped wetness as the marauding tongue tickled her sensitive sexual tissues. The juice first trickled then ran out of her in a stream of rising pleasure.

It didn't take long for Karen to climax. Afterwards, she stared dreamily up at the ceiling. Megan lay down beside her and kissed her, holding her tenderly in her arms.

Oh, how sweet—you'd almost think they were wife and wife, Jane thought. *At least Megan already came before I got here.* She checked her watch. It was 1 a.m—there was still sufficient time for her to get things done here and get back home and into bed for a refreshing night's sleep.

Now she just had to wait for the sisters to separate. She hoped that wouldn't take forever. She also hoped they weren't going to fall asleep all lovey-dovey here. That would mean her performing her operation here. She could do it, but a bed was better for surgical procedures than a coffee table was. Neither was perfect, but a bed was wider and she could also maneuver more around the 'patient.'

The girls finally separated. Or rather, Megan got up off Karen, who'd passed out after climaxing. The younger woman lay there, mouth open, snoring.

Megan, meanwhile, staggered over to the coffee table, took one final swig of bourbon, and then headed off to her bedroom.

Jane padded after Megan. She watched Megan enter her bedroom, noted that she'd left her door ajar, then hurried over to peek through the crack. She was in time to watch Megan flop down on the bed on her back. Megan began snoring too.

After slipping a shoe into the crack of Megan's bedroom door to ensure it didn't click shut in her absence, Jane returned to the living room. Time to put Karen out of action. Though the girl seemed far gone in her alcoholic odyssey, Jane couldn't take any chances. It was very possible for Karen to wake up suddenly and decide she wanted another orgasm and come looking for Megan.

Jane stood over Karen for a moment, studying her open mouth. The girl had really nice teeth, very white and even, and with very few fillings.

Too bad one can't eat teeth.

Jane pulled one of the hypodermics out of her pocket. Karen had a large number of visible veins on her hands. Jane selected the fattest of these, rubbed it with an antiseptic wipe, and injected the drug. She'd used a very tiny needle, almost a baby-needle. Karen probably felt the prick as a bug biting her, if she felt it at all.

That took care of Karen then. She'd be in guaranteed dreamland for the next three hours at least. More than enough time to do the dirty deed.

Jane returned to the bedroom, to Megan, whom she'd really come to visit. Megan had been too drunk to turn the lights off. Her slumbering repose on the bed once again afforded Jane a fantastic view of her profile.

"Too bad I'm not a lesbian," she murmured to herself. "I'd have loved to push those lips and that nose between my legs."

Enough reflection. She stared at her target. Megan was still lying on her back and breathing deeply. All Jane needed to do was give her the same shot she'd given her sister, and then she could begin. Both injections were identical, so she didn't have to bother with remembering which was which.

She got out the unused hypodermic, then looked Megan over, wondering where best to inject her with it. Her hands? Her arms? Unlike her sister, Megan was fleshy, a vein would be more difficult to find. Jane wondered whether she should get the chloroform from her bag. That would knock Megan out long enough for her to take her time with putting her properly to sleep.

But then, staring at the drunk woman, Jane was struck by an idea:

The way Megan Morgan had fallen onto the bed—she'd simply backed towards it until it hit her knees and then let herself drop—had left her left leg dangling over the bedside. Her right leg was up on the mattress, spread wide and bent at the knee, with the sole of her foot pressed flat on the white bed sheet. What this did too, was spread Megan's vagina wide open.

Jane stared at the drunk woman's vagina. She stared *into* it; that recently-sexed hole still lightly creamed with white. Suddenly she felt excited.

Jane had once read about how the legendary jazz singer Billie Holliday used to inject heroin into the veins of her vagina. Jane had always wanted to try out something similar, just not on herself. Here now seemed the perfect opportunity.

The most tricky part of injecting Megan in her vagina wasn't locating a nice, suitably throbbing vein (Jane was, after all, an expert on human anatomical science), but how not to wake her up while parting her labia.

She considered knocking Megan out with a hono nerve pinch, but then decided not to. Considering how drunk Megan was, she was uncertain what the side effects of the martial arts technique would be: such an unplanned, additional depression to her system might prove fatal—she had no intention of killing the girl.

She decided to handle this the harder, straightforward way. She could always knock Megan out with brute force if she woke up during the procedure.

Jane finally got it done—spread the young woman's sexual lips wide apart, got the needle into the tender vagina, and forced the syringe's pale contents into its wet side tissue.

Then she waited for three minutes. After that, she took the chance of forcefully shaking Megan Morgan.

Megan didn't bat an eyelid. Jane shook her again. Megan seemed dead.

Alright, that works a treat, Jane thought. *Next time I'll try injecting the sedative into that fat vein that runs down the top of a man's penis. It's strange how drug addicts never try shooting up there—it's like the fattest visible vein in a guy's body. All you need to do is jerk off and then—bang! But then, who wants abscesses on their cock?*

While thinking this, she was descending the stairs to retrieve her two suitcases.

Once back upstairs, she opened up both suitcases, put on her green surgical gown and white surgical mask, and slipped on her latex gloves. She always wore gloves to protect herself. She was wary of contracting AIDS or hepatitis.

It was now 1:26.a.m. Give or take a few minutes, she was on schedule.

She surveyed her equipment, in this case mostly scalpels and a little electrosurgical kit to seal off bleeding arteries. This latter she'd plugged into the bedroom wall socket and grounded under Megan's body with a dispersive pad. In addition, she had swabs and forceps and clamps, along with other miscellaneous tools. Everything she needed.

***

Jane cut deeply around Megan's face. The scalpel sank into the pink skin, then parted a red gutter through it.

Blood spilled. Jane stopped cutting, swabbed and cauterized; the spark of electricity and the slight smell of burning flesh. (She could have used the surgical pencil for cutting, but she preferred the feel of steel against her fingers. There was just something brutally perfect about dipping a knife into another person's body; this act of freeing blood from skin seemed a preview of how she'd later consume them and make them an inseparable part of herself.) When a stubborn vein in the girl's temple kept dribbling even after she'd tied a ligature around it, she stitched it up in a fold of skin to prevent excessive bleeding.

She resumed cutting. Because of the wealth of muscles and arteries involved, a facial operation required intense concentration. Also, there was no way to tourniquet the woman's head without asphyxiating her.

Jane worked tirelessly, wishing she had a nurse to mop her brow like one always saw being done on TV. Occasionally she'd stop to wipe off some blood that had squirted up onto her face because she'd loosened her surgical mask and let it dangle around her neck. Her sea-green scrubs already had several red patches on them. (Despite her concern about catching a disease, Jane had an aversion to surgical masks. She liked smelling her patient's spilling blood, and to her mind, the masks interfered with this.)

Every now and again she'd take half a minute or so off to ensure that Megan Morgan was comfortable. It was alright: Megan was breathing evenly, no shock as of yet. For respiratory emergencies, Jane had brought along a gas mask fitted with a compact oxygen cylinder. But so far Megan didn't need it.

Jane resumed work. Cutting, separating, cauterizing, ligating, and all the while anticipating how delicious the flesh would taste. Once, when Megan stirred and moaned through what was left of her mouth, Jane gave her an additional shot of painkillers. Almost as if she was grateful for the consideration, Megan sighed loudly then relaxed again. Jane got back to work on her face.

By 2:45 a.m. Jane was finished. She studied her handiwork. Yes, it was definitely a little messy, with maybe too much blood splattered around Megan's head and mingled with her black hair, but she'd not killed the girl, and most important of all, she'd gotten what she'd come for, that precious meat now secured in the small icebox she'd brought along in one of her suitcases.

Satisfied at a job well done, Jane packed up her tools and cleaned herself up in Megan's bathroom. She made a final check on Megan's vital signs, decided she'd be okay after a little intramuscular shot of adrenalin, administered it, and then left the bedroom.

Before descending the stairs, however, she made a pit stop in the living room to give Karen a follow-up shot of her own; just something to wake her up in about an hour. That way Megan wouldn't be in any real danger. Jane was certain she'd correctly followed all the procedures for minimizing blood loss, but one never could tell—she might have missed some teensy-weensy blood vessel somewhere which, if left untended, might kill Megan.

So best that Karen rouse her sister.

Jane left at 3.05 a.m.

CHAPTER 15

Ghost

That same night, at about that same time:

Ghost got naked and had a bath. She took her time with soaping herself, getting herself all clean for the ritual of skin.

***

This was another *In The Flesh* night at club Safe Word. Ghost had missed the last one. After the TULIP meeting held in her house that evening, where they'd decided to begin an investigation of Insane Jane, she'd no longer felt in the mood for sex. The scary knowledge that the woman lived in the same city as she did had murdered and eaten her arousal.

But this was three weeks later. She definitely was in the mood now.

Still, she'd arrived late, not stepping through the club doors till 3 a.m. because she'd been finishing a search for a client—this time for a long-lost friend who wasn't on social media. She'd located the person, closed the case file, and decided she needed to relax. And for that, there was really only one place to go.

Safe Word was open all night. She merely had to arrive there.

***

After bathing, Ghost examined the selection of women's masks that were available tonight. At Safe Word, everyone wore a mask, even couples who'd arrived together. Everyone became a depersonalized body, an organ for the pleasure of others.

She chose a plain pink 'spook' mask and donned it.

Nine minutes later she was chained to a frame in the Whipping Room with a muscular man in a horse mask lashing her. Her hands were secured above her head, her feet similarly spread so that her body formed an erotic 'X.'

The whip cracked, her skin tingled; welts rose and blood flowed. She grit her teeth and bore the pain.

"Harder!" she gasped.

Ghost trembled under the lash. It was always the same: at first there was just pain, but then the pain transformed into arousal, a deep dark excitement she wouldn't exchange for anything else; and each succeeding lash thrilled her flesh, each touch of the whip now feeling like she was wrapping herself in silk, until finally it overflowed and the release came, like water being poured over her.

Around her, other naked people, both men and women, were giving into similar sadomasochistic impulses.

Ghost came, then slumped on the rack. The sensations burned deep in her skin felt as if she'd just been freed from herself.

"More?" the flagellator asked. Looking back, Ghost could see pre-come swinging from the man's swollen penis.

"Enough," she replied. "For now, at least."

"As you wish," he said politely and crossed the circular room to where a musclebound man was waiting for someone to beat him into ecstasy. He began whipping the man.

Ghost had little time to relax herself. Almost immediately, a busty brunette wearing an orange fox mask and high-heeled red thigh-length boots was slipping a strap-on into her ass from behind.

"Ouch," she gasped as the dildo filled her rear passage.

"I knew you'd like it," the brunette whispered, pressing her breasts hard against Ghost's back. "I'm gonna fuck your ass so good, baby, you'll never have trouble taking a shit again."

Ghost sniggered. "Tough words, bitch, but can you fucking deliver? Lotsa guys been back there before you and I still regularly get constipated."

"Oh, I'll make you a believer in my cock."

The plastic penis seemed to be penetrating into Ghost's bowel now.

She grunted and took it. It hurt, but if you didn't like pain, what were you doing in an S&M sex club?

While thrusting, the brunette licked the blood from Ghost's back. Not advisable, in Ghost's opinion; but some people didn't care if they picked up a disease, or gave you one.

"You taste wonderful," the woman said.

When she was done, Ghost turned to look at her. She was surprised to see that the woman hadn't been using a dildo like she'd thought—she actually had a penis. The organ was still hard and throbbing. Also, the condom she had on was empty—she hadn't ejaculated yet.

The chestnut-haired woman took a few more licks of the blood on Ghost's back, kissed her on the ear and departed across the room, where she was soon chained to the wall herself and receiving a hard flogging from a very thin and barefoot woman wearing, of all things, a snake-head mask.

"Release me," Ghost instructed one of the attendants. These wo/men were all dressed in striped crotch-less pants and wore zebra masks.

The attendant immediately released her. Once freed, Ghost crossed the Whipping Room and stared at the brunette transsexual who'd just penetrated her anus. The woman was squirming under the lash. She'd removed her condom and pre-come was dripping from her erection, the dangling thread of clear liquid swinging left and right in time with her large testicles as she wriggled with each beating. Both her back and her buttocks were a webwork of red lines.

"Hit me like you love me!" she gasped. "Make me feel the strength of your emotion!"

Breathing hard from the effort, the woman flogging the transsexual now concentrated on beating her buttocks.

"Take that, you fat-assed cocksucker!" she mocked, landing her black cane strategically across the left ass-cheek, making her victim grunt and thrust violently forward as though the air around her naked and stiff penis was a tight and wet hole in someone else's body.

The woman hit the reddened buttocks harder. Ghost watched and rubbed herself towards a second orgasm.

"Oh, God, yes!" the transsexual brunette groaned, then ejaculated from the force of the pain alone, without anyone touching her penis or anus, the sperm shooting out like white bullets and splattering the wall.

Moaning and fingering herself hard, Ghost gasped out her own climax.

When Ghost recovered from her orgasm, she walked off to seek yet more stimulation. Both she and Safe Word were far from done. The middle of the night was still young.

CHAPTER 16

Jane

Jane drove carefully away in her black van.

Unwilling/unable to use a vehicle's mirrors to view the world behind her, Jane had evolved an alternate system. Mostly she used her ears (in a way similar to a bat's in-built radar). Other times she peeked back through the front seats while driving. She calculated when to do this based on her relative position to the vehicles beside and in front of her. In any case, to date she'd not been involved in any crashes.

Occasionally, a loud noise from behind her car would tempt her to at least use the central rearview on the windshield. Normally, she resisted the temptation. Sometimes though, she didn't. Most of those times too she was lucky and saw nothing amiss.

Other times . . .

No, using the mirrors wasn't worth the nightmare hassle.

***

A few minutes after leaving the Morgan house, Jane passed an open 24-hour store with a grocery section, at the Commonwealth Street junction. She suddenly remembered she needed to buy some eggs for breakfast. The all-nighter seemed as good a place as any to get some.

She considered not stopping. It was very late/early, and, now that the excitement of getting her fresh meat had worn off, she felt dog-tired. She looked at the dashboard clock. 3.10 a.m. She had just enough time to catch some sleep, though she'd need a lot of coffee—and some scrambled eggs on toast—to perk herself up before work.

Look, screw this and just go home. Buy the eggs at work! Soon the police are going to be out looking for you! Yes, they have no idea who you are, but d'you wanna help them find out?

Not stopping was the logical step to take, which was the reason Jane didn't do it. Instead, she slowed the black van and looked around for somewhere to park it. It would be silly to U-turn and drive it back to the store. No one there must see the van. No one must be able to link her with the vehicle.

As she cruised, she noticed a building on her right, set a little back from the roadside. She turned towards it, turning off her lights as she did so. She remembered this place, an abandoned four-story building that used to be an old folks' home. It was scheduled for demolition, but the city hadn't yet gotten around to knocking it down. Most important though, the building had an underground garage—the signs pointing to it were visible from the road through the surrounding tree fence of dogwoods and maples. One could also see the building's empty windows, most of them now devoid of glass and looking like the eyes in a corpse's face.

Behind the old building, some heavy construction was going on. From Jane's previous glimpses while driving past, she thought a hospital was being built back there. Or maybe it was the replacement old folks' home.

Whatever the case, here was perfect for her to park for a few minutes.

She drove down the concrete ramp, parked, and then switched her headlights on again for a brief look around. Aside from herself, the underground garage was deserted. Rows of concrete pillars and some graffiti: 'D.O.A' written in white and red, and shadowed with blue.

Jane killed the headlights. She turned on the interior light and had a quick peek into the van's rear, at her two suitcases, one of them containing the cooler of face-meat.

A cold smile of delight on her face, she got out of the van and locked it up. Slipped the keys into her pocket.

Almost immediately, she found herself surrounded. The figures had materialized from the reestablished shadows as if they were ghosts. She trembled slightly, feeling fear for the first time tonight.

Someone flicked on a torchlight and she was able to make out the figures as young men. Five of them, dressed in leather and denim and carrying knives and chains. All in their late teens or early twenties. They had the hard ruthless faces of gang members and drug users.

Oops, Jane thought, *stopping here was a bad idea after all.*

Two of the boys put on cellphone lights.

"Hey, sweets," the leader said, "looks like this is our lucky morning, don't it?"

"I don't want any trouble," Jane said, acting the part of the scared female. In actuality she was far from scared. There were *only* five of them. They'd be easy to handle.

The leader laughed. He was tall and quite big, with long dirty-blonde hair and a 'heavy metal rocker' mustache and beard. He clicked open his switchblade and waved it at her. "Neither do we, sweets," he said. "Just hand over your pussy nice and easy, and we'll let you be on your way."

She felt she needed to make some kind of stand. "My name isn't 'Sweets,' " she growled. "It's Jane."

He laughed again. Each time he spoke, his voice seemed to leave his mouth, echo all around the subterranean garage, then return to him. "Oh, yeah? And here I was trying to be all gentlemanly with you. Well, *my* name's Thugg, bitch, and you'd better spell that with a double 'G.' Just in case you don't get it—you're trespassing on D.O.A turf here, and we don't take kindly to bitches, or anyone else for that matter, walking into our house uninvited. Dig it, bitch?"

If he calls me a bitch one more time! She bit back an angry retort. In situations like this one must keep one's cool. "So, Thugg with a double 'G,' " she said, "what do you want with me? It's three in the morning, and I gotta be getting home to bed."

It was hard to keep a mocking tone out of her voice. Already he looked slightly perplexed that she wasn't afraid of him. And she wasn't. She looked around the gang members. The problem now was that she'd have to kill them all. She couldn't have any witnesses describing her to the cops afterwards.

"Bed? Oh, we got a bed for you upstairs," one of the other boys said. "A nice soft one your ass is gonna love."

Jane's biggest regret was that she wouldn't have the time to harvest any choice meat from these young men after she'd sent them to their deserved early graves. She was too tired now for surgery and if she left the corpses here and returned for them tomorrow night, the meat wouldn't be as fresh as she liked it to be. And there was also the possibility of someone else driving down here to park just as she had, and their discovering the bodies.

What a waste, she thought. *Well, they're a bunch of waste products anyway.*

Jane had no sympathy for rapists. She hated them. To her, rapists were the scum of the earth and deserved everything they got. Jane, who liked sex as much as the next woman, always cringed with disgust whenever she read of some poor woman who'd been mercilessly molested by hooligans. Hooligans like the ones who wanted to defile her now.

After killing these particular hooligans, she thought, *I'll just relieve them of their testicles—they won't need those down in Hell.*

Yes, she'd cut off all their balls. Meatballs! Not their penises though. Penis was very tough if one didn't cook it right, and so far, she'd not yet perfected her recipe.

The gang leader was staring at her. It was as if he could read the death script playing in her head. He was trying to figure her out.

"Hey, Thugg, what're you wasting time for? Let's give this slit some dick like she'll never forget in her stupid life. I mean, in her afterlife." The speaker was a skinny dark kid in a wife beater shirt. A really nasty piece of work. Pockmarked face and missing some teeth. But he had lovely eyes.

Oh, you cutie pie, I'm gonna carve out your eyes and roast them, she decided there and then. It was a pleasant thought. After she'd killed them all, removing this boy's eyes along with everyone's testicles wouldn't take her long.

The other young men were meanwhile laughing at her. One already had his penis out and was stroking it.

"And she's so frigging pretty too," the skinny boy said. "Hey, Thugg, for fuck's sake, what the hell are you waiting for? Let's put the blocks to her."

Thugg silenced him with a sharp gesture. "Cool it, Bulletface. I'm running this fucking show, not you."

Then laughing, he pointed to two of the other young men who hadn't yet said anything; the two who weren't masturbating. "But still, Bulletface, you're right. Alright, Rod, Jack, grab the bitch and let's take her upstairs to the pad; let's give her the hard time of her life."

Jane relaxed as they approached. Then, as they grabbed at her, she moved, twisting and flexing her body. Grip and throw. The young man on her left went over her head and smashed into the side of her van. The one on her right howled in pain as she twisted his arm behind his back, ducked behind him, and kicked him in the back of his knees so that he went down kneeling in front of her. Next, she grabbed him firmly around the head.

But then, a split second away from breaking his neck, she stopped. She let go of him and kicked him forward onto his belly.

Reason and caution had just overcome her lust for blood. She'd just seen more young men stepping out of the shadows. And two of them were holding guns. Guns with homemade silencers attached.

That didn't work, Jane thought. *Looks like I won't be killing anyone tonight.*

Before she could do a thing about it, Jane found herself surrounded again in the underground garage. The boy whose neck she'd almost broken had rolled over onto his back and was gasping for air. The one she'd thrown against her van was back on his feet, holding his head and doing his best to keep the others between her and himself. The one who'd been fondling himself had hurriedly put away his member again.

"Hi, baby," the leader of the new arrivals greeted. He was tall, with dark hair, and might have been handsome except for a long scar down his left cheek. Looking at him in the torchlight/phone-light glare, Jane felt a sharp surge of hunger in her belly. As was normal when she scouted male prey, the hurt felt sexual. She thought the boy looked delicious with all those bulging young muscles. Oh, how she'd love to have his abs in a skillet.

"Jacko, guys, this is Jane," Thugg introduced. "She's the pretty but feisty bitch who'll be entertaining us all tonight."

"I'll scream," Jane said. "I'll call for the cops." Her body pose, however, was far from a cringing one. She stood relaxed but poised for a fight. No one else stepped near to her. The newcomers had also seen her self-defense skills.

"Be our guest," Jacko replied. "But know this: if you scream, we'll kill you and fuck your corpse. Just so you know, 'D.O.A' stands for 'Dead or Alive.' "

Jane was certain he was bluffing—who except crazy people had sex with corpses?—but she decided not to put it to the test.

"What do you want?" she asked, to buy time. It was as clear to her as the night outside the parking lot that sex was all they had on their silly young minds.

Haven't they already told me as much? They just want to fuck me, and maybe kill me afterwards.

Thugg grinned. "We already told you that, bitch, but I'll repeat it as you seem hard of hearing. We want *you*—that tight ass and wet pussy you're hiding in your panties." The others assented with loud masculine murmurs. "Unwilling as we know you'll be, Jane, you're going bareback riding with us tonight for sure."

Jane considered her options. Assuming her van didn't currently contain Megan Morgan's severed face, she might have raised a fuss. But not now. In addition to the iced-packed human flesh in her vehicle, there was also the question of the *number* of these young men.

There were ten or twelve of them around her; maybe up to fifteen even. Too many to go Jackie Chan on, even if the new arrivals hadn't had guns. There was no way she could kill all of them without being wounded herself, which, even if they didn't kill her, would mean her leaving a sample of her DNA here. Yes, one knife stab or bullet wound could immediately undo everything she'd spent so much time and care setting up, unravel her carefully spun feeding web. And if she didn't kill them all, the escapees would be able to give her description to the police, as well as the number of her vehicle.

So, no more fighting. She intended to put up no more resistance, except if her life was being threatened.

At the moment, Jane saw no alternative to her being fucked by all these young men. She'd finally counted fourteen of them. None of them over twenty-two years old, yet all with penises desperate for her thirtyish body.

I wonder what it is that teenaged girls don't have nowadays.

But then, putting her genius brain to work, Jane began figuring out how she could turn this disadvantage to her advantage:

What can I get out of this? How can I use this? she thought. *How can I use these boys? They're young, dumb, and full of come. They're malleable. All I need is to bend them to my advantage.* It was an interesting puzzle, one Jane found all the more amusing because she knew the young men didn't suspect a thing. *They imagine they have power over me, when right now I'm about taking their wills over and twisting them to my superior purpose.*

Time for Plan B . . . no Plan XXX. She looked around at them all, daring them with her eyes.

"You guys, grab her hands and legs and carry her upstairs," Thugg instructed some of the others. Next, he pointed at Jane. "And, lady, remember—you try any more of that goddamn Kung Fu shit and you'll get a bullet in the back of your head."

"Wait!" Jane said in a commanding voice. "I wanna say something."

Everyone froze. The tone of voice she'd used had had something of 'Mother' in it. All men respected 'Mother.' Even those who hated her. Even those who murdered her. Jane stood there, illuminated by the glow of cellphones and flashlights and dared them to resist her compelling will.

She shook her head at Thugg. "Don't bother holding me down. I'll give you all what you want." She smirked, taunting him. "You want me? You can have me, and willingly at that." She stared the one named Jacko cold in the eye. "But I get something in return."

"Bitch, we don't have to give you anything," Jacko said. "We'll just take your ass for the trespass."

"And afterwards, we'll kill and bury you," Thugg agreed, clearly annoyed that she wasn't scared. "No worrying DNA evidence that way." The sounds from the other boys confirmed their agreement with their leaders. These others were a hydra-headed shadow, with the red glow of cigarette tips as the seal of their communal presence, and the reek of marijuana smoke their animal pack odor.

Jane squeezed her breasts at Thugg. She flashed her teeth disarmingly at him, a creamy erection-inspiring grin that in reality promised nothing at all. This was psychological warfare: get deep into your opponents' pants and make them dependent on you for their goals in life. Sexual domination. Control them. Control them.

I must and I will control them. I am a goddess. They are young fools.

"Yeah, yeah," she said in a bored voice, "so you can force me to fuck you all. But how much fun is it gonna be for you guys if I'm kicking and screaming and you have to knock me out so that it's like you're all fucking a corpse, huh? Except you're into necrophilia, it can't be that great." She struck a defiant, but very sexy pose. "It'll be much better if I'm a willing participant in this gangbang. And I can be—I'll be your very own porn star—but I want something in return."

Though not in the least bit promiscuous, Jane was a mistress of the art of seduction. The confidence with which she spoke made an immediate impression on the gang members. She hid her satisfaction. Young men were so easy to control.

"Hey, and I ain't talking about money," she added before they got the wrong idea about her.

"Yeah?" Thugg asked. "Alright, what do you want?"

She gestured around. "Are you guys always here?"

"What's that to you?" Jacko asked, then took a swig from a bottle of whiskey someone had passed to him.

"I mean, can I find you lot here if I need you for something?"

Thugg regarded her coolly, clearly wondering if she later intended to bring the cops over to their hideout. But he saw something crazy in her eyes that said different.

"What kind of something are you—"

"Hey, bro, what's all this shit!?" the kid named Bulletface interrupted loudly. (Jane had forgotten about him.) "Thugg, Jacko, are we gonna be yapping with this silly skank all night, or are we nailing her ass to a fucking bed? Man, I got a big nail right here in my pants— eight inches long and fat as a stripper's pole."

"Shut up, Bulletface, you half-wit!" Thugg growled back. "I've already told ya—I'm running things here, not your anorexic junkie ass. The lady says we can all have her, and that she'll do it willingly, so I don't see what difference a two-minute delay makes. I like this woman: she's feisty like my mom. I wanna hear what she's got to say."

"Well, I don't," Bulletface grumbled back. "I don't give a shit about—"

Thug looked pained. "Somebody, please shut this skinny son-of-a-bitch up. And I mean *permanently*."

It was almost poetic, Jane thought. Like a scene acted out on stage, Jacko instantly pulled out a knife and stuck it deep into Bulletface's neck. Then he jerked the knife forward and out so it left a huge hole.

The stabbed boy looked shocked for a moment, then, gurgling blood, he sank down to his knees and died. The other kids stepped away from the blood spilling from him.

Jacko shrugged, wiped the knife clean on Bulletface's hair, then straightened up and took another swig of whiskey.

Thugg nodded at Jane. "So what were you gonna say?"

She nodded down at the dead kid. "Aren't you worried about the police finding his body?"

Thugg shook his head. "Nah, there's a construction site right behind us. They're building a hospital for old people. By this time tomorrow he'll be an inseparable part of the foundations. My older brother Ralph works there so we won't have no problems getting rid of him."

The one named Jacko spat whiskey down onto the corpse, then scratched the scar on his face. "No one'll miss this son-of-a-bitch. We were gonna kill him anyway—we just found out he's been snitching on us to the po-po. My kid brother's in jail now 'cos of him. He was most likely goading us on to rape you so he could film it and pass it on to the cops."

He passed the whisky bottle back to the boy he'd gotten it from then frowned at Jane. "Alright, out with it, pretty woman. What kinda assistance you want from us?"

She in turn frowned down at Bulletface, who lay cold and staring in a still spreading pool of red. She thought of the eyes and testicles she'd planned on taking from him. But of course, she couldn't request for them now. She mustn't give away any clues that might later lead to her.

She didn't realize she was licking her lips. Some of the gang saw her do so. Those kids assumed she was merely thinking of all of their hard penises penetrating all of her soft holes.

"Oh, you know," she responded airily, while at the same time undoing her belt. "The streets ain't safe nowadays. Occasionally a woman can get into some violent trouble and might need a little help"—she gestured down at the dead boy again—"disposing of the evidence down a pile hole."

Thugg stared at her in surprise. Then, seeming to sense a kindred violent soul, he smiled and nodded. "And, do we get more pussy in payment?"

She shook her head. "Hell, no. Tonight's a one-off. My pussy can't take all you guys on more than once. You'll get cash. I'll pay you *very* well for services rendered. I promise you won't be disappointed with the money." She cocked her head and peered inquisitively at Thugg. "Deal?"

Thugg first looked across at Jacko for his approval, then he nodded at her. "Alright, deal then."

She stepped out of her jeans, then began undoing her top. "Alright, boys, who's first?"

Thugg shook his head. "Not down here in the parking lot. In the clubroom upstairs. Nice and comfy up there."

"One more thing. You guys got condoms?"

"Condoms? Hey, Thugg bro, what is this shit?" a deep voice asked out of the darkness. "Are we screwing this uppity bitch or what?"

Thugg looked at Jane like he was uncertain. "For fuck's sake, lady, just spread your legs for the guys and stop talking B.S."

She tried again: "Hey, just listen. I know I'm clean, and I can tell from looking at you that you are too. But what 'bout these others? You wanna pick up someone else's diseases?"

Jacko laughed. "Fuck condoms, Jane. Us in D.O.A? We're the Bareback Riders Suicide Squad. Everyone's gonna die someday. Better if a man dies of pussy-related causes than a cop bullet."

"Damn straight, fire-crotch," a blonde-haired young thug agreed. "You just donate that red-haired pussy of yours to us and we'll worry about what horrible diseases you're carrying."

"Alright, let's do this," she stated coolly, "I need to be at work early today."

She gave a mental shrug. There was nothing for it then. She'd have to do it bareback. She'd already figured they wouldn't have any rubbers on hand, and none of the gang looked willing or smart enough to walk to the 24-hour store down the road to buy a box of condoms for safe sex.

"Hey, no one's gonna mess with my van in the meantime, right?"

A laugh: "Don't worry 'bout it, lady. Bulletface's corpse'll keep watch over it for you."

"Great. Let's go upstairs, boys."

Thugg raised an eyebrow. He was super impressed by how cool she was.

Ah, so I'm about to be gangbanged, Jane thought without emotion as the group of young men led her across the underground parking lot and up a set of spiral stairs. *Well, I guess I had to have some bad luck someday. Better this horny lot than the police. At the very least it'll be quite an experience.*

Jane's primary worry at this point was that she'd not put enough ice in the icebox, and that her freshly cut face meat might spoil if she spent too long having sex.

***

The gang took Jane up to an apartment on the third floor and there had their way with her.

She was stuffed everywhere—ass, vagina, and mouth (she'd never before imagined one's tongue could feel rubbed raw from sucking so many penises)—and the penises were of different shapes and sizes. Most weren't clean either. The uncircumcised ones were particularly dirty, with the gang members seemingly having a competition on as to who could produce the most and the smelliest smegma.

Jane's biggest problem during the gangbang wasn't the pain or the soreness, however, but the overwhelming urge she felt to bite down on each penis that entered her mouth. Not because she was angry, but because all that hard meat was making her hungry.

D.O.A fucked Jane *really* good.

CHAPTER 17

Karen

As if a donkey had kicked her in the heart, Karen Morgan came awake abruptly. Placing trembling fingers on her breasts, she felt her heart beating rapidly.

Yes, I was dreaming, but no, it wasn't a nightmare. I was actually sucking some guy's horse-sized dick and loving it. So how come I woke up so suddenly?

Her head felt unsteady on her shoulders.

She stared guiltily over at the coffee table. *Oops, we did it again—Meg and I got shitfaced and fucked each other!*

She felt both satiated and disgusted. This—she and Megan's incest—had been going on for so long now that Karen couldn't remember any longer which of them had started it. Ever since their teen years this had been the trend for them: once she and her elder sister were between boyfriends they sought satisfaction in each other's arms.

Karen got to her feet. *Well, we'd better grow up. We gotta stop doing this. Or else, one of these days someone's gonna catch us at it. And then we'll really be screwed. I'll discuss it with Meg in the morning. It's gonna be hard for me to give up sucking on those fantastic tits of hers, and she eats pussy like a porn star, but . . .*

She scowled and said aloud: "But right at this moment, I gotta pee something awesome."

Her heart still pounding fast, Karen stumbled out of the upstairs living room. Her bedroom was at the end of the hallway. Megan had the nearer room. Megan's door was wide open and she'd left her lights on.

Karen detoured towards Megan's door. Best to close it for her.

But then she stopped in Megan's doorway and froze.

99

Megan was in bed, with her chest rising and falling rapidly like she was in pain. But what was scaring Karen (and making her racing heart beat even faster) was that Megan seemed to have some kind of huge insect squatting on her face. The bug was bulky and black, like a giant roach or beetle.

A bug? Karen stopped her intended reaching for the light switch and stepped inside the room instead. With nothing else to swat the giant bug with, she picked up Megan's laptop.

Now armed after a fashion, she advanced towards the bed. Her heart pounded with alarm. All she could think was that her elder sister was in danger.

Where the hell did a bug this size come from? Wha . . . wha . . . what the hell is that!?

Karen froze again. She'd just noticed something else. She'd been mistaken.

No, that isn't a giant cockroach on Meg's face. It's a frigging gas mask! It's been modified though, that's why it confused me . . . The bottom half of the gas mask was a small black tank, which, due to the series of silver tubes connecting it to the main unit, lent the whole thing its eerie similarity to an insect.

And hey—why the hell is there so much blood around Meg's head?

Now Karen was really worried. Her older sister was still jerking as if she was having trouble breathing. But other than that she wasn't moving at all. Her arms and legs lay limp as boiled noodles. It looked like she was having a heart attack.

Her hair and shoulders were covered with congealed blood.

Yeah, Karen nervously agreed with herself, *breathing difficulties would explain the mask, but where did she get it from? I've never seen it before. And why didn't she wake me up first?*

And the really worrying question now: *Why the hell is Meg bleeding from her head? Did she fall on something?*

Karen stepped right up to the bed and carefully put the laptop down beside her sister's legs. Megan would be mad if she damaged the thing.

Then she bent over Megan's head and, reaching carefully behind her older sibling's bloody black hair, she removed the modified gas mask.

This proved to be much more difficult than Karen felt it should be—the gas mask felt stuck to Megan's head.

Finally though, Karen got the gas mask off Megan's head.

Then, struck speechless by disbelief, she dropped the mask and froze for the third time.

Where's her face?

Megan no longer had a face, or for that matter, any flesh at all above her chin. No, that was incorrect, Karen slowly realized: she did have some flesh left, but the majority of it had been expertly scraped away, leaving just the skull, with two staring gray eyes. The entirety of Megan's facial skin was gone. She had no nose anymore. Nor any lips either, just bloodied teeth and jawbones remained, jawbones so bare of flesh now that Karen could see the underside of her sister's tongue through the space in the bottom of the lower one. Megan's cheeks were holes in her skull. Like furniture viewed through a house's windows, her tongue, gums, and bloodstained soft tissues were all visible inside the wreck that had been made of her head.

Both of her ears were also missing.

What Karen was looking at was a skull stripped of almost all its flesh—everything between the hairline and the top of the neck. But, Megan still had her scalp and all of that long and glossy hair that Karen had so often admired and envied. Around the fringe of her hair, a surprisingly small amount of blood trickled. Indeed, the whole operation which had stripped Megan of her face had a touch of intense perfection to it. Intense perfection tinged with intense lunacy.

Megan was clearly still asleep. Her lidless eyes were staring up, but in vacuity—they revealed no awareness of her mutilation. Her chest heaved erratically, but her labored breathing apparently had no connection to the mess that had been made of her.

How? How? How? The question filled Karen's mind like the strident buzzing of angry bees. *How? How? How? WHO? WHO? WHO? WHO THE FUCK DID THIS TO MEG!?*

And right then, as though prodded by Karen's anguished mental questions, Megan jerked awake. Suddenly her eyes moved in their sockets. Mercifully, the psychopath who'd butchered her had left her eye muscles intact.

With a hand stuffed in her mouth to stifle the screams threatening to burst forth, Karen watched her sister; watched while she tried to blink but found she couldn't. Watched her raise her hands to her head and feel herself. Knew that she was baffled, but lacked the face to reveal that confusion.

There was a moment of silence, when Karen felt as if the world had stopped spinning, though her agitated heart was beating as hard as if it was the engine spinning the world. Then Megan's previously 'just woken up' stare abruptly transformed into a look of impossible-to-convey terror.

Next, a series of heartrending noises spilled from her jaws: "GWUUUUBLLUU! GGIIIIIIIHHHH! GAAADDDUUUSSSAA!"

It took Karen a moment to realize why Megan sounded so odd:

She's screaming, but without any muscles left in her jaws, she can't open her mouth to properly let out the sounds!

Megan screamed on and on. Her unnatural noises in turn set off something inside Karen: a flood of undiluted fear that welled up from the depths of her guts.

Karen began screaming too. Screaming and urinating at the same time.

CHAPTER 18

Jane

Hard young bodies, cruel faces, eyes that flickered with amoral desires.

The gangbang finally ended, to Jane's relief.

She peered at a clock on the wall, then gasped. It was past five, almost dawn. Outside the windows, the sky was lightening.

What? We've been at it for two whole hours?

The time had passed for her in a blur of swollen male organs and the occasional orgasm for herself. Occasionally one of the boys had held a tray of coke and a straw under her nose. Her black wig lay over on a table, discarded the first time one of the gang had grabbed her ears to gag her with his penis. Similarly, her black lipstick had all rubbed off on turgid gangster erections.

They'd used up an entire large tube of sex lube on her. A full tube. Thank heavens it had been watermelon-flavored lube. Each of the thirteen surviving gang members had had her at least twice. Several of them had even fucked her three or four times. Her belly felt so full of semen now that she didn't think she'd be eating anything for several days. The last guy in her ass had come so much in there that when he'd pulled out of her it had felt like she had diarrhea.

Still . . . she surveyed her spoils of war, the multicolored battleground of tattooed male flesh, disheveled hair, and the combined stink of semen, sweat, human dirtiness, and her excrement on their penises.

Looking around her at the young men strewn across the room like discarded clothing, she saw that she'd triumphed in this battle of the sexes—her vagina had worn the whole gang out; a grand statement on the power of a woman. She was standing; all thirteen young men were exhausted. The D.O.A members lay in different positions around their clubroom. Several, like scar-faced Jacko, were already fast asleep. Thugg was on his back on a couch, smoking a joint and staring at her with awe.

He saw her looking at him too and nodded. "You definitely delivered on your promise, Jane."

She nodded back. "I can leave now? Or you wanna go again?"

Thugg gaped at her and groaned. "What the hell are you? A nympho-demon sent to kill us all? Friggin' go home and kill your boyfriend instead!"

"Yeah, biatch, go home!" someone else groaned from the floor. "We don't like you no more."

She laughed. "And the other thing? My end of the deal?"

Thugg waved a hand. "It's still on. Just call me when you need us. Good money, right?"

"Definitely."

Thugg nodded and went back to smoking his joint.

Jane walked past the sleeping young men into the bathroom.

Oh, she was as sore as hell—it hurt to walk and she doubted that she'd ever pass feces or swallow food again in her life—but her agreeing to give them what they'd been about taking by violence had meant that (except for a few playful slaps on her buttocks and breasts) she'd not been hit even once.

She'd worked out that as a sexual maneuver, ass-to-mouth wasn't recommended anywhere outside of porno flicks. Nor was ass-to-vagina. She'd very likely need to take a course of antibiotics to stem any resulting infections.

She'd also discovered that double penetration—both anal and vaginal (and oral too)—was a total no-go area for her.

Her breasts felt like they'd been mauled by a lion.

It had been quite the experience. However, she wasn't repeating it. Not for all the money in the world.

My first gangbang and most definitely my last!

***

After showering, dressing, retrieving her wig, and getting Thugg's cellphone number, Jane staggered to the door. From there she waved back at the clubroom—"Bye, boys, the fucking was nice, but now this nice girl's gotta get the fuck home"—and found her way downstairs to her parked van.

Before climbing into the van, she stared for a few moments at Bulletface's corpse, wondering whether or not to relieve him of his eyes and testicles like she'd initially planned on doing.

Finally, with an audible sigh of regret, she decided it really wasn't worth it:

Some of those D.O.A gang kids are on drugs. After a bust they could easily tell the cops about this 'weird chick' they'd once met, if they think it'll make the law go easy on them.

She got into her van and drove off along Hamilton Street. By now the first of the day's cars were already on the road.

Damn, she thought. *It's almost five-thirty and I'm out on my damn feet. I'd better just call in sick today. Raw as my crotch feels at the moment, there's absolutely no way I can stand behind that checkout counter for eight hours.*

CHAPTER 19

Ghost / Jane

It was half-past-five when Ghost left Safe Word. Relaxing behind the wheel of her red Mazda she felt sated. As she drove, the pain from the floggings she'd received seared her back and ass and thighs, reminding her of the pleasure that had accompanied each lashing. In addition, the pain teased her with tendrils of future expectation, the desire for more of the same.

The sex had been really good tonight. Despite the lateness/earliness of the hour, Ghost felt energized, ready to go back to her normal life, to her everyday job of finding things for people. Without a tormenting flood of sexual impulses to distract it, her mind was as clear as the road ahead.

She felt as charged as a battery.

She turned the car radio on, tapped the tuner buttons to find some music.

On the third change she caught part of a news bulletin: ". . .This is Mark Mellow on the Early-Bird Show. Alright, listeners, now for something gruesome . . ."

Ghost quickly cut the man off, switching to a music station playing a Barry Manilow song. She didn't wish to hear anything gruesome. At the moment, she felt too good to be brought down by another person's misfortunes.

***

"Alright, listeners," the man on the radio said, "now for something gruesome: Reports are just coming in about an attack last night on a woman in Worcester in which her whole face was stripped off her head while she slept, seemingly with surgical equipment. The victim is now known to be Ms. Megan Morgan of . . ."

Jane smiled at the news. While Mark Mellow gave details of the Morgan sisters' house, she glanced behind her at the suitcase with the meat cooler in it.

Despite my aching pussy and ass, it's been a good night.

She'd just arrived at the I-290 overpass over Grafton Street. She looked forward again, saw that the traffic light at the northbound I-290 turnoffs (which intersected Grafton) had turned amber, and slowed her van to a halt.

***

The Barry Manilow song finished. Ghost didn't like the next song on the show. She turned off the radio. She felt around in the space between the seats for a CD to put in the player. She took her time with this; the light up ahead had just turned red on her and several 18-wheelers were crossing Grafton Street from the I-290 turnoff.

She finally found an old Astral Leftovers CD and slotted it into the CD tray. She clicked the music on and leaned back again. Once more the pain in her back and buttocks cuddled and caressed her.

"Hey, so I think I'm going crazy,
Solid things are turning hazy,
And the world is spinning round me.
My brain is playing mind games with reality,
'Cos I'm seeing stuff that can't be . . ."

The traffic light was still red; more trucks were crossing the intersection. The sun was coming up fast now, the sky lightening in quick stages through shades of gray to the new day.

Ghost looked out of the passenger side window at the vehicle on her right, a black van with a raven-haired woman behind the wheel.

She smiled. The woman was very attractive. She looked exhausted though, as if, like Ghost, she wasn't just leaving home, but instead returning to it after a long night's work. Occasionally too, she winced in pain as if she was really hurting somewhere.

I wonder if she too was at Safe Word tonight. It isn't an impossible coincidence.

The woman seemed to sense that someone was watching her. She turned towards Ghost. Sensing a kindred BDSM soul, Ghost felt friendly enough to wave at her.

The black-haired woman smiled. She looked as though she might have waved back, but then a spasm seemed to grip her in the belly and she looked away from Ghost again.

Yeah, Ghost thought sympathetically, *she looks completely exhausted. And the way she's wincing, maybe she's having period pains.*

Ghost looked forward. The last of the vehicles in the intersecting lanes were past now and the road ahead was clear. The traffic light should turn green any second now. Foot poised on the gas pedal, she glanced across at the woman in the van, hoping she was alright.

And then, out of the blue, something really weird happened. All of a sudden, there wasn't a beautiful woman sitting behind the wheel of the black van any longer, but instead, a large white rabbit. A man-sized rabbit with a mean expression on its bunny face. Like a man wearing a furry party costume, the white rabbit gripped the steering wheel in a pair of huge paws, its pink eyes staring straight ahead.

Ghost gaped in confusion. *What the vagina fuck?*

But by now the traffic light had turned green again and the huge white rabbit drove the black van away across the intersection.

Ghost sat perplexed, shivering with fear. She remained parked where she was, not moving her car even at the honking of the angry drivers behind her. She didn't even notice them driving past her, or hear their shouted curses.

What the vagina fuck was that? she wondered in alarm. *What the vagina fuck did I just see?*

PART 2: A RECURRENT HUNGER

CHAPTER 20

The Bay State Problem That Wouldn't Go Away . . .

It wasn't that the Massachusetts State Police didn't know they had a problem with Insane Jane, their problem was that this problem was one they had no solution to.

The cops had a stack of case files but no real leads of any kind. They'd investigated, but found nothing.

No clues, which considering at least thirty people had so far been attacked, seemed preposterous. But there it was: the cases stacked up, and if anything the evidence got slimmer and slimmer. Each time the trail vanished at the victim's front door.

She left no traces . . .

Strangely, instead of simplifying the investigation, the fact that no one had yet died actually made things more difficult for the police. Most of the 'survivors' didn't wish to call attention to themselves and their mutilations. There was no glamor in losing an arm or a leg during one's sleep, waking up to find oneself butchered like a side of lamb. Such a misfortune smacked of carelessness even. It was better to tell friends and family that one had lost one's leg (or arm, or kidney, or liver, or ears) in a car crash or an accident at home.

The classic case of the latter was the man, who on calling 911, claimed to have slipped and stuck his entire right arm down the kitchen disposal.

Either way, the end result—amputation—was the same.

The flip side of this lack of public exposure was that no one was coming forward with leads. Which may or may not have existed anyway. The press played up each crime as it occurred, but with no apparent rhyme or rhythm to the attacks—sometimes there were up to six months' gap between them—even making a positive linkage between Insane Jane's surgeries was difficult.

It was a peculiar case. After a while, even the news reports seemed to reek of the fantastic, like something the National Enquirer would print. No one really believed (or wanted to believe) in something as outrageous as Insane Jane's graphic displays of brutality.

Were these all the work of just one deranged woman, or was this merely a new, especially nasty sort of crime, one that waxed and waned with the seasons? Something with twenty or more different perpetrators?

The police wished it was the latter, but suspected it was the former.

The Massachusetts police also wished that the woman called Insane Jane would do everyone a favor and move elsewhere. They didn't care what state of the union she went to, just so long as it wasn't in New England.

She?

Even the idea that Insane Jane Doe was actually a *woman* was suspect . . .

CHAPTER 21

Jane

The woman was quite fat. She was maybe in her late forties, was an ash-blonde, and had large gray eyes. Quite beautiful eyes. She had a small nose and a large red mouth. Neat teeth. Because of the cold morning weather, she wore a knee-length gray coat over her white dress. Her massive bosom stuck out between the flaps of the coat.

Something about the fat woman made Jane think she knew her from somewhere. Possibly the way she had of looking around nervously as though she felt people were staring at her ass. Then she'd tap her fingers on her shopping cart handle as though keeping beat to a song.

As the woman unloaded her cart onto Jane's checkout counter that chilly Tuesday morning, Jane took proper stock of her. Her huge breasts. Her breasts seemed to be propped up by her equally massive belly, which was in turn propped up by the handle of her shopping cart.

I want her, Jane decided without hesitation. *I'm going to have her. Oh, I gotta have these boobs on a plate.*

***

It was now ten days since her last trip out when she'd been gangbanged by the boys.

The primary aftereffect of the gangbang was that her orifices still hurt. All she'd given her boyfriend Scott this past week were hand jobs, with a few grudging flicks of her tongue on the head of his penis just before he came—no full-insertion-into-mouth fellatio; the inside of her mouth was still too sore for penile contact. She'd explained to Scott that she'd picked up a toilet infection and didn't wish to pass it on to him. She'd told him the antibiotics she'd been prescribed would clear the infection within another week, after which "my holes are all yours again."

Some 'morning after' pills had ensured she'd not fallen pregnant with a gangster baby.

But, on the plus side, Megan Morgan's face had tasted utterly delicious roasted. The meat had been juicy and tender, the nose cartilage nice and crunchy. Jane had fried Megan's facial skin in butter and made sandwiches from it. Scott had loved the taste of those.

***

The fat woman, oblivious to Jane's thoughts, was looking around again.

Jane tallied up her purchases. (Today she was at Checkout Counter 8.) Detergent and bath soap and sponges and bleach and a whole lot of canned food. No pet food, but she was also buying a lot of ice cream, butter and meat.

Maybe she had kids, maybe she didn't. Jane didn't care either way. Just those breasts. Those stupendous breasts that seemed to be attacking her with their graphic prominence.

I want them and I'm going to have them.

Jane began salivating. The thick liquid pooled in her mouth. She had to swallow fast and keep swallowing.

"That'll be $169.36, ma'am. Cash or charge?" she said politely, trying not to stare at the impressive mammary carriage. This would be easy; the woman qualified for the Bahamas Cruise competition and looked like the sort who enjoyed traveling.

The woman handed Jane a credit card. Her name was Lara Hutch. Jane swiped the card.

"Ma'am?" Jane tried to hand the woman's card back to her.

The fat woman hadn't heard Jane. She was totally distracted by something. She was staring down into the store, away to Jane's right, towards the liquor section.

"Excuse me, ma'am . . ." But the woman still didn't turn towards her. Whatever she was looking at had a headlock on her attention. The customer behind her, a black teenaged girl who was the spitting image of Nicki Minaj and who was wearing headphones with the music turned up loud enough for Jane to hear the hip-hop she was listening too, seemed in no hurry either. The girl was nodding to the hip-hop beat and blowing large chewing gum bubbles, each of which she then popped with her long black fingernails and sucked back into her purple-colored mouth.

"Hey, ma'am, your . . ." Jane began speaking to the fat woman again, but then instead turned to look at what had captured her interest.

That was a mistake.

Jane never saw what the fat woman was staring at. Instead . . .

The turnoff to the store's electronics department was just a few yards away from Jane's counter. A woman had just walked out from there. The woman, who was tall and slender and looked like a model, turned towards the liquor section. At the same time, she opened a large compact and began checking her face in its mirror.

Like a pest drawn to poison, Jane's gaze leapt at the mirror. The angle was wrong to catch her own reflection, but she caught a flash of something. A brilliant 'something' that streaked out towards her before she could look away again.

Shit! she thought as that 'something' hit her in the brain.

Suddenly Jane was falling . . . falling back through the years . . . completely unable to halt her descent . . . or alter her final destination . . .

CHAPTER 22

Jane In The Past – 2

Jane was eight again, and back in the burning car with her family roasting around her. Her mother—her hair and clothes brightly aflame—was screaming and trying to climb out of the sunroof opening, but each time she attempted exiting through there, flames poured in at her, almost like they were fingers pressing her down to her death.

Beside Jane, her brother Jimmy was already a charred lump of coal. But Jane herself . . .

Something was keeping the little girl alive and safe. True, her shoes were on fire, but her dress wasn't; and neither was her hair. The seat next to her was burning, and outside was burning also, but *she* wasn't. Still, the little girl felt like she'd once imagined a steak in an oven felt. Hot, hot, hot. And the thick black meat-scented smoke was absolutely choking her.

Jane had no idea that she was safe. Mother had fallen over between the seats now, her hair all gone, her scalp cracked open like hot desert rock and blood boiling out of it, her eyes gaping while her face blackened and imploded. Mother had stopped screaming. Now she was just gasping while clawing at the air with flaming fingers.

Jane was horrified. She was choking and crying and howling. She knew she couldn't remain in the burning car for long, or she'd end up like Mother and Jimmy. Her legs had begun really hurting.

And then, she saw it again: the rabbit, the same one that she'd earlier seen flying towards her to rescue her. A huge white rabbit.

And then the rabbit was right beside the car and was pulling the rear door off. And suddenly there was a hole where the door had been, and cool air rushed into the car and little Jane was lifted out. Safe and sound and unburnt.

The rabbit carried Jane away from the flames. He set her down under a roadside elm tree that stood a good distance off from the heat.

And it was only now that the little girl got a good look at her rescuer. She was surprised, so surprised in fact that in the wonder of what she was seeing, she both instantly stopped weeping and forgot all about her dead family:

Young Jane Winters had not been rescued by a rabbit at all, but by a man with a rabbit's head. Yes, he had paws for hands, but other than for that and his head, he seemed quite human. Her rescuer was tall and broad and wore a black three-piece suit with a gray-and-white-striped shirt and a red tie. His shoes were a brightly polished black and had shiny silver buckles like old-time pirate shoes had. His head was large and white and furry, with an albino rabbit's pink-and-red eyes, and his nose was pink and wet and his whiskers long as licorice strings or spaghetti.

His bunny ears were very long. As he put her down gently on the soft roadside grass, they bent like sails fluttering at sea.

Jane looked the rabbit-headed man up and down in wonder and asked him: "Who are you, sir?"

He grinned at her, baring thick white teeth, his large eyes shining with delight. "Oh, I'm Mr. Floppyears, young lady. Yes, Mr. Floppyears at your service." He had a nice cartoon-rabbit voice that filled her with confidence and trust. He leaned forward towards her. "Are you alright, little one?"

"Yes, sir."

"That's good then. That's real good, little girl." Mr. Floppyears straightened up and looked back towards the burning sedan. "Oh, it's so bad that we couldn't save your family though, but I'll go have a look anyway. There might be something we can salvage from the wreckage . . ."

"Don't go, you'll get burnt up too!" Jane yelped.

But Mr. Floppyears was already heading back towards the burning car. He walked in a funny way, like he was both hopping and running at the same time, and while he walked his two-foot-long ears kept bending left and right like tree branches in a high wind.

Jane watched him in wonder. The non-dazed portion of her young mind was trying to understand why . . .

Before she could understand what she was trying to understand, the little girl felt herself being hauled up through the years again. And as she was pulled up through herself, she grew older and taller and smarter and heavier and . . .

CHAPTER 23

Jane

"What happened to me?" Jane asked on opening her eyes again. She was lying on a bed somewhere.

"You fainted at your checkout station," Caroline Chen replied. "We were going to call for an ambulance, but then you began mumbling about giant rabbits. So Matt and Donnie carried you in here to my office instead."

Slowly, Jane made sense of things: *Shit, I had that memory of Mr. Floppyears rescuing me again.*

She hadn't had that flashback in years, but then, she'd not looked in a mirror—not directly anyway—in three years. For makeup, she merely rolled lip gloss over her lips and she was done. Everyone told her she looked pretty. She'd seen enough pictures of herself to realize that her friends weren't lying about her good looks.

Damn the damn mirrors. Damn Mr. Floppyears.

Jane noted her current position. She was lying on a camping cot set up in a corner of Mrs. Chen's office.

She saw that Mrs. Chen was staring down at her worriedly. Caroline Chen was the new head cashier/cashier supervisor, a middle-aged, calm and very sensible Chinese lady. The previous supervisor Mr. Ackerman had been transferred to Ohio to head up the first Cashstretch branch there.

Jane sat up. "I'm sorry about this happening. I haven't been sleeping well lately. For some reason I just feel so drained today."

"I understand." Mrs. Chen handed Jane a bottle of water. Bent over Jane like she was, her black hair hung like curtains beside her oval face. "How do you feel now? Do you think you need a doctor?"

Jane shook her head. "No, I'm alright now. It was just . . ." She couldn't tell the older woman that it was her glance at the mirror that had done it. *Two times out of ten,* she remembered. *Eight glances that I take in a mirror are fine for me, but those other two . . . It's best not to look in them at all.*

Now Jane felt fine again. She felt her energy returning.

"You seem really weak," Mrs. Chen said. "I think you should just go home now. Yes, I think that'll be best for you."

"But . . ." Jane protested. "I'm fine. I'll be alright now."

"No," Caroline Chen said firmly, walking back over to her desk and leaning on it. "Go home, Jane. Go take some rest, and if you still feel ill, see a doctor, either today or tomorrow morning. In fact, take tomorrow off as well and, please do make an appointment to see a physician. I'll have José cover for you."

Jane saw no point in protesting.

"In fact," Caroline Chen said, "I'll have José drop you off at home first. You didn't bring your car to work today, did you?"

Jane got up from the cot. "Oh thanks, but it won't be necessary. The walk home will do me good."

The new cashier supervisor shook her head sternly. "I insist. I don't want you collapsing on the street."

Jane was about objecting further—she really felt wonderful now—when a question came to her mind: "Er . . . Mrs. Chen, how long was I out for?"

"You've been lying there for about twenty minutes."

Oh shucks, Jane thought, a look of dismay spreading over her features. *The fat woman must have left by now!*

***

José Fernández dropped her off at home.

Once he'd driven off again, Jane got down to thinking: *Lara Hutch—I need to find her. I need to find that woman. I just have to get her! Her home address is surely on the contest form she filled in.*

Then she considered further: *But did she even fill in a contest form at all? In the confusion after my faint, no one would have remembered the contest. Dammit! How do I find her? How in the heck do I find her? Those breasts! Those breasts!*

The thought of Lara Hutch's breasts got Jane hungry. She headed to her kitchen fridge and got out the last of the sandwiches she'd made from Megan Morgan's facial skin. The delicious crunchy texture of

Megan's fried skin—so much better than chicken skin—filled Jane with delight and helped her think.

So how do I find that woman? There's no way she's escaping me!

It was quite the puzzle.

CHAPTER 24

Scott & Jane

Scott came over to dinner that night. While Jane cooked, he sat in the living room reading the Worcester Telegram & Gazette.

"Hey, honey," he called out when she stepped out of the kitchen for a few seconds, "you're not gonna believe this story that I just read."

She paused and stared at him. "What about?"

He grimaced at her. "It's just utterly horrible what some folks do nowadays. This is just nasty."

"Scotty, I can't read your mind. What is horrible and nasty?"

His face all twisted up in revulsion, Scott replied, "This story: a girl here in Worcester—Megan Morgan—just committed suicide."

Jane didn't let her shock show. "What's so odd about that, sweetheart? People kill themselves everyday. It's the modern form of psychic protest—I'll off myself to show you how pissed off I am with *you*."

"You don't yet know *why* she killed herself, or *how*."

"Sorry, you're right. I'm listening."

"Apparently, two Sundays ago someone cut her entire face off."

"Ugh. How'd I miss that on the news?"

"I recall hearing a rumor of this at work, but I was too busy to ask for details. And now this . . . Anyway, whoever it was cut off her entire face, all the skin and muscles, and her nose and lips and ears . . ."

"In the daytime?"

Scott shook his head. "Middle of the night. Cops think it happened around 2 a.m. Apparently, from this article, all that he left her was just the bones of her skull and her eyes—the psycho apparently wanted her to see how badly he'd mutilated her."

"Hey, wouldn't that kill her?"

"Apparently not."

"So, how'd she die then?"

He grimaced again. "Gunshot wound."

Jane's eyes widened in surprise. "Huh? Gunshot?"

"Yeah. It says here in the paper that Megan's younger sister sneaked a gun into the ICU yesterday and Megan blew her brains out with it."

"Oh, that's really a tragedy," Jane said with heartfelt sympathy. She hadn't intended for Megan to die. She'd intended for her to live. Even though, now that she considered things realistically, maybe she'd been overoptimistic about the young woman's future prospects. If you stole someone's face, what did you leave them to live for?

Okay, I'll stick to body meat from now on. I don't want any more deaths on my conscience. Poor girl. Oh, what a pathetic end to your life, Megan!

"Do the police have any leads?" she asked Scott.

He shook his head. "They're worse than baffled. There's a suggestion that this is linked to a similar case out of town—some guy who woke up in the middle of the night with his legs missing—but that's all. They've no suspects yet."

"Hmmm," Jane said. "This reminds me of what Caitlin and I were discussing the night she came over with you. I mean, about those three women who went missing last year. The world's just crazy now, sweetheart." Jane let a tremor enter her voice now. "I can't blame that girl for killing herself—if something that horrible happened to me, I don't know what I'd do."

Scott put the paper down, and came and took her in his arms. "Don't worry about it, honey. I'm certain the cops'll find the culprit soon."

"But . . . but . . . you just said yourself that they're clueless."

"Oh, it doesn't matter. They'll keep after him until they do find something. The guy's certain to slip up sooner than later. Psychos always do."

With her face buried out of sight in Scott's chest, Jane laughed silently. Scott though, thought she was crying and gripped her tighter and stroked her hair soothingly.

Not this one, sweetheart, Jane thought coldly. *Not this one, Scotty. But then I'm not crazy anyway, darling. So I'm clearly not going to get caught ever.*

She pulled back from him. "Thanks, darling, I'm fine now. Oh, hang on, I need to check the soup." She ducked into the kitchen, calling back over her shoulder: "And, hey, how's Caitlin doing anyway? Have you spoken to her recently?"

He leaned against the kitchen door. "Yeah, yesterday in fact. Oh, that reminds me—Janie, I've a favor to ask you."

"A favor?" She turned away from the gas range to face him. Now she was smiling. "Ask me anything you like."

He smiled back at her, glad that she'd recovered her spirits. He felt it had been silly of him to have read out that horrible news story to her. "It's nothing serious. Just that this Saturday is Caitlin's twenty-fifth birthday and I'd like her to celebrate it with us. Preferably here at your place."

Jane thought on it a bit. "Sure, that'd be wonderful. But what about her friends? You said she has a boyfriend."

Scott rolled his eyes and flung up his hands. "Oh, you mean Stu? Those two are on and off so much you'd think they were a pair of light switches. They're apparently 'off' again at the moment, and I was thinking that us—you really—having Caitlin here to dinner would give the girl a nice sense of being loved and wanted. You know, a sense of family?"

Jane wiped her hands on a green napkin. She giggled understandingly; he was so easy to see through. "Scotty, sweetheart, by now I know you very well. You're trying to get me to bribe your daughter into liking me, aren't you?"

He grinned broadly back. "Better earlier than later, right?"

She nodded. "Yeah, sure, why not? Let's have her over here. I'll cook up a birthday storm for her."

Scott took her in his arms again. "Thanks, honey. Oh, this is one of the reasons why I love you so much."

She giggled. "You're welcome. Just don't start calling me 'honeybunch' like you do Caitlin. That's cringeworthy."

He kissed her tenderly on the lips. "Okay, I promise not to, honeybunch."

Jane laughed and pulled back from him again. After playfully punching his chest, she said: "Hey, man, if you love me so much, where's my damn engagement ring?"

He laughed too. "Oh, it's on its way. I'm saving up for a really big one."

"How big are we talking about here?"

"Oh, the biggest diamond ever. Just you wait and see."

***

Much later, after giving Scott his hand job for the day, she posed him a question:

"Sweetheart, you work in a bank, so you should know about this. Okay, how would you go about finding someone?"

"What kind of a someone?"

"A friend."

"Facebook."

Jane altered her position on the bed so that she was sitting up facing him, while he lay on his side with a contented look on his face. "Yes, yes, I know that. But how would you go about finding where they lived?"

Scott gave her a queer look. "You'd just ask 'em?"

"Yes. But if they were all cagey-like, and . . . okay, view it this way: A girl's chatting with a guy online. But she's not sure if he's really a guy at all? Or she's not sure if he's just playing her for a fool? You know he could be married and just stringing her along. Or he might be an identity thief trying to rip her off, see? So she wants to find his personal information."

He looked at her even more queerly. "Hey, you aren't cheating on me, are you, hon? I mean, I ain't had this many hand jobs from girls since high school."

She scowled. "No, Scotty, I'm not fucking cheating on you. Answer the question, please."

Scott shrugged. "Hire a hacker. That's what I'd do. Once you know the guy's name, a hacker should be able to dig up personal stuff about them. I think you'd also need some other info though, like a car number or credit card or social security number, or, if the person has told you where they work. Stuff like that, so the hacker can be sure they've got the right person—you know how there's lots of people with the same name."

He was shocked by Jane's sudden predatory grin. "Yeah, that's what I was thinking too," she said.

"But," he quickly cautioned, feeling worried by her sudden enthusiasm without knowing why, "hiring a hacker is a two-edged sword. Sure, they'll likely find out everything you wanna know, but you'll also be compromising your own online security too." He regarded Jane closely. "Honey, you wanna wake up one morning to discover your bank account has been drained empty?"

She shook her head. "No, but I don't think I've drained your balls empty yet. So, how about another wank?"

Scott rolled his eyes. "You're really enjoying tormenting me like this, aren't you?" He reached up a hand and cupped one of her full breasts. "All this gorgeous expanse of stacked redhead and all I get are the fingers."

"Count yourself lucky, baby. At least you aren't getting fingered, or getting the finger."

"Yeah, well there is that. Yes, darling Jane, I'll gratefully accept your gracious offer of another dose of gratuitous masturbation. Hey, how about the hacker we were just discussing?"

"Oh, screw the hacker. I was just curious, that's all. New girl at work has that problem and we were discussing what she could do. I don't think I'll advise her to hire a hacker though, not with the personal risk to herself." Jane faked a shudder. "And not on considering that creepy story you told me about that poor girl's face. Who knows where the psycho got her address from?" She reached down between Scott's skinny, inedible thighs and grabbed his penis. "And now, let me just take this dick of yours in hand. Wow, it's getting big!"

"C'mon, honey, suck it a little. Just a little bit?"

"Not till this weekend, Scotty boy. The sex will make Caitlin's birthday a double celebration for us. Until then, hands it is!" She began stroking his erection firmly, her other hand cupping and gently squeezing his testicles.

"Ooh, Janie," he groaned, "you wank me so good, honey!"

CHAPTER 25

Ghost

That same night:

The handsome young man blew her a kiss and left. About time too. Sex with him had been good, but once it was over she'd felt crowded in, wanting to be alone with herself. He'd seemed to sense this. Anyway, he'd left her his phone number. She'd hook up with him again next week, on another off night. His cunnilingus was really up to par. Her vagina tingled sweetly now with the memories of his tongue flicking across and inside it.

Ghost got out of bed. She stretched. She walked into her kitchenette and got herself a beer. Then she sat down at her computer desk and woke up her main laptop from its electronic slumber.

She felt like doing a little work. Nothing serious, just a guy's find request for a college sweetheart. The client had no idea if the lady in question was dead or alive—she'd apparently vanished last year, and no one had the slightest clue as to her whereabouts now.

Ghost studied the woman's picture. A large but pretty blonde. Colleen Townsend. She was married, but her friends all said her husband Larry was cheating on her; so there may have been foul play involved in her disappearance.

Ghost suddenly found herself remembering her weird experience of two Sundays ago, that morning when she'd been driving home from the Safe Word meeting: the woman driving the black van who'd suddenly transformed into a giant bunny before her very eyes.

She sipped her beer. No need to be silly now—she'd just been tired then and hallucinating. Women don't turn into rabbits!

She knew that to be true. Yes, she hadn't seen what she'd seen. Despite which, Ghost had been intrigued by the incident every since. What if she wasn't hallucinating that morning? What if she did actually see that happen? What if she'd just unearthed another urban legend for TULIP to investigate?

She liked the thought. For one thing, investigating the bunny-woman would be a whole lot less dangerous than investigating Insane Jane. Rabbits didn't eat people; that was the plus side of this.

She'd told the other TULIP members about the bunny woman. She'd suggested they switch their investigation to her instead. Ninja had stoutly refused. She felt pissed off with Ninja now. Like all guys, he thought he knew better than she did.

"You know the rules, spooky one," he'd told her via webcam, his fat all-encompassing grin making him look like something unnatural that needed investigating. "Once agreed on, the quest can't be altered. You voted in agreement to that rule too."

"But . . . it's *dangerous*? Did you hear the news about the girl whose *face* she cut off?"

"Yes, I did. At the moment I'm hacking into the Worcester police databases—trying to dredge up what they ain't telling we the helpless public. That's another victim in this city. We're pretty close to our prey now, aren't we, Ghost?"

"Too close, man. What if . . . ?"

Ninja had beamed patronizingly at her, which had made her wish he was here in the flesh so she could break something over his head. "It's always dangerous, spooky girl. Like Warrior says: 'We do this for the thrill of danger.' "

"I don't."

"Too bad. And also too late. I'll suggest to the others that we look for your bunny woman *after* we're done tracking down Insane Jane. But Insane Jane it is for now. Deal with it."

"Vagina fuck you, man!" she'd growled. At that point she'd felt Ninja was just a fat patronizing dickhead out to get them all killed. Or worse still, get parts of them eaten.

He'd smiled condescendingly back. "Be hard to, baby. I ain't the pussy; you are." Still smiling, he'd terminated the connection.

That was that then. They were stuck with investigating Insane Jane. God only knew why she, Ghost, was the only one in TULIP who sensed how dangerous the woman was. (True, Avatar seemed worried too, but then Avatar was always worrying about something or the other.) To her mind, it would be best to let the cops find Insane Jane, but no, Ninja seemed to have a boner for the crazy bitch. As if he wanted to fuck her when they caught her.

A beep notified Ghost that she had a message on OTTmeet.

She looked at the screen name of the person messaging her and winced. It was Anna Jeisen, the elusive rich and hot MILF.

Ghost wondered what the hell the damn pussy tease wanted from her. And—she checked the time on the laptop screen—at three in the morning, for that matter. Anna had never messaged her at night before.

Nevertheless, she clicked open the message.

Hi, sexy biatch, Anna had written, *I need you to find someone for me.*

Ghost smirked. Big deal. Yes, she'd told Anna she found things and people. But the damn woman was just a tease. All talk and no fuck.

But . . . visions of Anna's big breasts swam through her mind. Ghost imagined having those large nipples between her teeth and nibbling on them ever so gently while Anna Jeisen gasped; sucking on them while she and Anna fingered each other to ecstasy.

She sighed. Fat chance there was of that ever happening. The old girl wouldn't ever screw. But still, she figured she had nothing to lose by replying.

She typed out a reply to Anna: *Hi, honey. What can I do you for? Unauthorized pussy eating, or tit violations?* Knowing Anna and her sexual repressions, the barest suggestion of sex should scare her off again for maybe the next six months.

Not this time though. Almost immediately, she got back a reply: *I'm serious. I need you to find someone for me. Her home address. Where she lives.* The reply came in so fast, it seemed almost as if Anna had already written it before Ghost replied her.

Oh? Ghost thought it over. Though one never said 'no' to money (and Anna was apparently very wealthy), anything Anna Jeisen wanted was certain to be more bother than it was worth. So no. Go away, pussy-tease!

She typed: *Sorry, Anna—but I really don't have the time. As I type this, I'm up to my pussy in 'search and locate' requests. In fact, some of the requests are searching locations inside my pussy* :-)

Another lightning fast reply: *Hey, do it for the money, biatch. I'll pay you two thousand dollars to find her.*

Ghost had a quick rethink. She couldn't turn down that kind of money. She'd be dumb to.

She typed: *Two thousand bucks? Anna, are you nuts?*

The reply flashed back: *No more than anyone else. I can afford the money. And . . . I'll sweeten the pot: You find out where she lives for me, and I'll not just pay you, I'll pay you in person.*

Ghost's reply expressed her surprise: *Huh? Pay me in person?*

Anna replied: *I mean, I'll give you the money face to face. Yes, I'll also agree to meet up and bump breasts. That's what you really want, ain't it? You can even use a strap-on and whip me too. You know you want to.*

Ghost pondered on that for a short while. She couldn't get Anna's breasts out of her head. And to actually fuck the hottie with a strap-on?

Alright, she agreed. *I'll do it. I'll find her for you, and once I do—your pussy is mine! So what's her name and what else do you know about her?*

***

Not much to go on. Just a name—Lara Hutch—and a MasterCard number. A description—the woman was blonde, quite fat, and had large breasts. Seemed barely enough to find anyone, but then Ghost wasn't going to be looking for Lara Hutch anyway.

She emailed the name, card number, and description to Ninja. She tagged it 'Urgent.' Even if Ninja wasn't awake now, he'd get right on it first chance he got.

Then, feeling like she was on top of the world, Ghost got down to looking for her previous client's vanished college sweetheart.

She had no success with finding the missing Colleen Townsend. That was normal enough. Sometimes people went to ground like rabbits: you had to dig them out little by little, cautiously, so they didn't bolt and leave you having to start searching for them all over again.

Ghost made herself some coffee. She sipped it, staring at the laptop screen, wondering in which of the USA's thousands of little towns Mrs. Townsend had chosen to hide herself.

She wondered what was up with missing fat blondes tonight.

At that exact moment, Ninja sent her a reply with an attached picture:

Found your girl. Mrs. Lara Susan Hutch. She's a widowed seamstress, with two kids away in college. She lives here in Worcester, at No. 195 North Lake

Avenue. That's on the east side of town, right by Lake Quinsigamond. Telephone number . . .

After the info, Ninja had added a question: *Weird request. What you after her for, anyway? I thought you didn't like us fatties. She don't seem the type you'd fall in love with.*

Beaming with delight, Ghost typed back: *I'll have you know I've dated several fat guys too. The sex was wonderful. I just got tired of them rolling on me in the night when I'm asleep. Each morning afterwards I'd be all flattened out and need inflating again :-) Thanks man,* she finished. *I'll send you your cut once I get it.*

Then she sat and pondered Ninja's question. She'd just realized that she didn't know the answer to it. Why was Anna Jeisen looking for this woman?

It was only now—an hour after taking on the commission—that Ghost realized that in her excitement over earning so much money at once and also finally getting to muff-dive into the gorgeous Anna's sex, she'd forgotten to ask Anna why she was looking for Lara Hutch.

She considered a number of worrisome possibilities, but shrugged them all off. Anna was much too timid and sexually repressed to be genuinely dangerous.

Ghost studied Lara Hutch's picture for a moment (yes, her breasts *were* massive), then forwarded the woman's contact info on to Anna Jeisen.

Then she sat back grinning and counting the days to her meeting with the beautiful object of her desires.

CHAPTER 26

Jane

1 a.m. Saturday morning.

Jane coldly regarded Lara Hutch's naked body. She had the woman spread out in bed, as neat and motionless as if for an autopsy. Expertly sedated and safely ensconced in a place where pain couldn't exist.

Lara Hutch had no idea what was hitting her.

Jane already had the left half of the fat woman's chest skin separated from her ribs and was now busy peeling the right half off also. Jane's main challenge with this operation was ensuring that she sealed off the main arteries supplying the woman's breasts with blood. At first there had been quite a lot of bleeding. But Jane had successfully isolated the blood vessels causing the trouble and tied them off.

The tiny capillaries and arterioles weren't any bother; she just needed to isolate the larger arteries that fed them. Veins weren't a problem either. She could easily distinguish those by their darker blood supply. Besides, blood only flowed one way through a vein: towards the heart. Once a section of vein had drained out its blood content up to the next valve, that was it; there was no backward leakage.

But the damn arteries. With those, a single slipup could prove fatal.

Now, as she hefted up Lara Hutch's left breast and folded it over on top of her right one, Jane was impressed by how heavy it was—it felt as heavy as a large puppy. It was juicy and fatty too. Excellent.

Jane stopped to take Lara's pulse. She tried placing a stethoscope on Lara's chest to listen to her heartbeat, but it stuck to the skinned muscle and sounded odd.

She wiped sweat from her brow, then sat beside her 'patient' and took a five-minute respite. While keeping her breathing regular, she stared at Lara's corpulent form, meditating on the fat woman's breasts; mentally accessing their calorific and nutritional value; visualizing them steaming in a pot as she boiled them down for their fat content.

At the moment Lara's torso looked like a bed that Jane was making up, as if the exposed flesh was the mattress and Jane just needed to tuck in that last corner by Lara's left shoulder.

Yes, there *was* a lot of spilled blood; but it wasn't anywhere near fatal.

She stared out between Lara's bedroom drapes, at the night stars. *Too bad the moon is on the opposite side of the house, tonight seems the night for it. Still it reflects on the water . . .* She looked down at Lake Quinsigamond instead, noticing two speedboats moored to the short pier beside the next house.

She considered too her being here tonight on such short notice. True, this was just three days after Lara Hutch's visit to Cashstretch, but Jane, never one to waste an opportunity (or stare a gift horse in the mouth) was striking while the iron was red-hot. She'd quickly realized that her faint at the cash register meant no one would ever suspect her of being Lara's attacker, no matter when she visited her. And also, seeing as she had Ghost to consider too, this had to be timed to absolute perfection. Thus tonight was just right for what she had in mind.

Then Jane had a sudden rethink. She decided to relieve Lara of her belly skin as well. She slipped off her bloodied gloves, got out a medical textbook from her bag, and began studying a colored anatomical map of the human torso. Just a quick refresher course. Every now and then, she looked up at the slumbering woman.

The old girl's gonna be overjoyed to discover she isn't fat anymore. Now, let me just remember where those damn arteries are . . . I don't want another death on my conscience! Yes, so for this artery here I need to calculate at least two inches deeper down from the skin because of her belly roll. Hmm, and I need to remember this one here too . . .

Her breather over, Jane got up, slipped on a fresh pair of latex gloves, and resumed her gory task. She stuck the scalpel back into Lara's pale flesh and slowly (more painstaking cauterization and ligation!) cut her right breast away also. Once she'd gotten both breasts free, she debated awhile whether it would be better to simply slice the freed breasts off and store them in her icebox (a large one this time) before continuing work, or whether she should instead keep breasts and belly together in one wide fatty sheet. She decided on the latter approach; that way she could just fold the woman's skin up—easier to handle like that.

She got to work with divesting Lara Hutch of her belly skin and its associated fat. Now she worked with a manic purpose. She'd become expert in the themes of her patient's body; she instinctively understood just how deep the scalpel would go before it stabbed into Lara's abdominal muscles. Thrice she correctly anticipated where arteries were before slicing into them.

The whole horrible gory surgery took Jane two hours to complete. (Oh, she definitely needed an assistant!) Once, she even thought she'd lost Lara. For the first time in years she came close to panic. She quickly put a gas mask on the unconscious woman and gave her a shot to strengthen her heartbeat a little.

But at last she could rest. Her surgery was a success. She had the entire skin off the front of Lara Hutch's body, rolled up like a Persian rug, and stowed away in her large icebox, and felt the thrill of satisfaction of a job well done.

She coldly regarded Lara. The woman was still out, her breathing shallow but regular. The front of her body looked like someone had ridden a lawn mower over her. Between pubic hair and shoulder blades she was a reddened expanse of bare muscle marbled with fat.

Partly to reduce on-site bleeding, partly for sheer esthetics (because staring at raw muscle like that seemed somehow wrong), Jane had, as much as possible, tried to leave a light layer of fat over Lara's muscles. But really, there wasn't much point to doing so.

Jane wasn't too bothered by how Lara looked now. With that exceptional brain of hers, she'd already done her calculations: Because she was so fat, Lara Hutch still had sufficient skin on her for the doctors to pull around to the front of her body and graft in place for a new chest and belly surface.

She'll be fine once she's in the ER.

Breasts? *Well, there are implants, and she'll have great fun choosing from the vast selection available.*

Nipples? *Hmmm. Yes, she'll look funny with fake breasts and no nipples. Her boobies are gonna look like balloons.*

She considered returning Lara's nipples to her: *Should I? Should I?*

But nipples tasted nice chopped up with onions, then roasted and smeared with cheese in a sesame seed bun. Scott thought so anyway, but of course he'd had no idea what he'd been eating.

No. I'll prepare the nipples as a special treat for Caitlin's birthday!

That was it then for Lara Hutch. After retrieving her gas mask from the woman's face (no point in starting a trend, leaving a gas-mask trail which the police might be able to follow), and leaving Lara's phone within easy reach of her hands (she propped it up on her belly with a bloody pillow), Jane picked up her cases and the filled icebox and departed.

Mission accomplished. She left, thinking she had quite a busy day ahead of her. Today was Caitlin's birthday, and there was also the little matter of her meeting the girl called Ghost to attend to.

She laughed, feeling a sweet thrill in her crotch. *Oh, I'm really looking forward to eating that young woman's pussy.*

But first of all, she had to go to work at Cashstretch. First shift.

She drove home, her black van becoming a part of the night.

CHAPTER 27

Ghost

3 p.m. Saturday afternoon.

As they'd arranged online, Ghost stood waiting outside the Palladium, on the corner of Main Street and Martin Luther King Jnr. Boulevard, smoking a cigarette.

Don't drive over, Anna had written. *I'll send a car for you. We'll be meeting at a friend's place, at least until we know that we're right for each other and I've worked out how to tell all my straight-laced friends that I'm dating a woman now.*

Ghost had readily agreed. She could practically read the nervousness typed in the words. *Wow, what a mouse this woman is. If she wasn't so pretty it wouldn't be worth it. And those great boobs she's got!*

The Palladium concert venue was just half a mile from Ghost's apartment, so she'd walked over, instead of driving and having to look for a parking space.

Ghost dragged on her cigarette and blew out smoke. That hadn't been all of it either; Anna's security precautions just went on and on: *I don't want anyone recognizing us, so please wear a red wig and . . .*

So now Ghost was dressed like a porno actress: red wig, heavy makeup with thick pink lipstick, jazzy sunshades; black jacket over a pink Slain Jane *Bitch Perfect* T-shirt; and a short red skirt that led down to black leggings and red peep-toed high heels.

I look like a hooker. The Saturday afternoon sexual matinee. The thought excited her. She patted her handbag. *Anna, I've got your strap-on right here. Once I get you into that bed, you're really gonna feel it, bitch.* The thought made her wet between the legs.

Her one concern now was that she didn't look too much the part, that a police squad car didn't pull over and bust her for soliciting. That would be just terrible.

Smiling at that possibility, Ghost tapped the ash from her half-smoked cigarette down onto the sidewalk. She next examined the pink lipstick ring on the filter. *Wow! Did I doll myself up for this or what?* Still smiling, she gazed across the road, at the shoppers opposite, wondering what they thought on seeing her waiting here.

They probably think I'm love for sale, she told herself.

Ghost was still musing on this when the large and obviously expensive brown Toyota SUV with tinted windows pulled up beside her.

The front windows rolled down. The young driver leaned across. "Miss Ghost?" he enquired. He was blonde and handsome and was wearing a black suit.

She nodded back and replied, "I'm real expensive, baby. Two thousand bucks per hour." This was the corny passphrase she and Anna had agreed on.

The young man smiled. "I'm Todd. Please get in the back. Mrs. Jeisen sent us to fetch you."

Us? Then the SUV's rear door was opened for her by another young man in a suit.

"I'm Jackson," he introduced himself, nimbly stepping down so she could climb in. He had an ugly scar down his left cheek. The scar marred his looks, otherwise he'd have been even better-looking than the chauffeur. It struck her that there was something 'rough' about both of these young men, but seeing as she was on her way to a sexual tryst, this impression merely excited her further.

Maybe these boys are even Anna's lovers. God knows the woman is too damn pretty not to be getting laid regularly.

Once she was seated, Jackson got in beside her.

She made herself comfortable on the plush leather seat. "Anna's really laying out the red carpet, isn't she?"

"Mrs. Jeisen says you're a special friend of hers," the driver said while putting the SUV in motion.

"She told us to give you our special treatment," Jackson said. "Our top of the range treatment."

Ghost felt nicely pampered. *Oh, but I do like the way Anna Jeisen rolls! The lady has class! This might turn out to be a nice relationship after all, something with a future.*

She turned to smile at the young man beside her and was shocked. Her smiled died on her lips. With a scowl on his face, Jackson was reaching towards her with a napkin in his outstretched hand. The napkin smelled funny, as if he'd spilled liquid on it.

She shrank back in fear. "Hey, stay back! What the vagina fuck are you doing!?"

And then he clamped the napkin over her face and though she tried fighting him off, she just felt incredibly sleepy instead.

***

Ghost revived in a large and dirty room somewhere.

She was lying on her side in a bed. Her hands were bound behind her. Her ankles were also bound. She was lying in a kneeling position, with her wrists tied to her ankles so she couldn't straighten out. She'd been stripped naked and her mouth was taped over with duct tape.

The two young men who'd abducted her were leaning over her. Both had now changed out of their suits and were clad in just their boxer shorts. Ghost was too terrified to admire their muscular physiques. The driver had a frown on his face. The other one had a hand inside his shorts and was stroking himself while ogling her.

They're going to rape me! she thought, her eyes widening in fear. *How could Anna do this to me? It surely can't be just because she can't afford to pay me!*

She had little time to ponder this though, because Jackson suddenly said, "Hey, Thugg, let's do this."

Her mind raced at the change of name. *Thugg? I thought his name was Todd?*

Scowling, Todd/Thugg picked up a switchblade from beside her bared breasts and flicked it open. "Yeah, let's get it over with. I got a hot date with Cindy."

No, don't! Ghost thought desperately. *No, Thugg, no!*

Her desperation increased when Thugg dragged her over to the edge of the bed. Looking down, she saw a small plastic bucket positioned right below her head.

"Hey, Jacko," Thugg growled, "stop wanking and help me hold the bitch down, wilya? Else she's gonna spill everywhere!"

"Oh, alright." Jackson pulled his hand out of his pants and grabbed hold of Ghost's legs instead.

Frantic thoughts filled Ghost's mind: *NO, this isn't happening! This is a nightmare! I'm dreaming! I'm dreaming!*

But then Thugg forced her head into position over the bucket and slit her throat deftly with his switchblade knife and Ghost was forced to realize that she was dying.

WHAT THE VAGINA FUCK IS GOING ON!?

CHAPTER 28

Thugg & Jacko

Thugg held the young woman's neck in position and watched the bucket slowly fill up with her blood. At first the red liquid jetted out, but then its flow ebbed and he had to tell Jacko to lift her legs up to ensure they drained her as much as they could.

The dying girl's bleeding paralleled her fight for her life. At first she bucked like a horse, but soon she weakened, and finally she seemed to accept the inevitability of her death.

The more blood that comes out of her, the less of her there is left, he thought. Thugg wasn't smart enough to be philosophical; this was merely an observation.

Thugg felt nothing for this girl. She was just a source of income. Jane had said the girl was blackmailing her and she needed her taken care of. She'd paid he and Jacko a lot of money—$15,000—to kill the girl, and they needed the money. All they'd had to do was rent the SUV from out of town and also hire a pair of tuxes. Jane had told them there was no danger; the girl would be disguised, so no one would ever recognize her afterwards.

So . . . bye-bye, blackmailing bitch. Peering out of the window beside the bed, one could see the construction site for the new old people's hospital, into the foundations of which the girl's body would shortly be absorbed.

Thugg smirked. *Come tomorrow morning, it'll be as if she'd never existed. She'll vanish as completely as that goddamn snitch Bulletface did.*

When it didn't look like there was much blood left inside her anymore, Thugg let go of her. She was long dead by now and her head lolled over the side of the bed as if she was merely drunk and the blood in the bucket was red puke.

Thugg stepped back from the bed and regarded the amount of blood. A little bit less than a quarter full. He wondered how Jane had known how much blood the girl would bleed and what size of bucket to use to collect it. He crossed the deserted D.O.A clubroom to fetch the red plastic can he was going to turn the blood into. It was a one-gallon gas can.

When he turned around again, he saw that Jacko had his boxers off and was leaning over the dead girl.

"The fuck you think you're doin'?"

Jacko leered back at him, the expression distorting the scar on his face into a zig-zag. He was stroking a throbbing erection. "Dude, I just wanna see if necrophilia's all that it's made out to be." He shrugged at his friend, then gestured down at Ghost. "Don't blame me, man. She's a fucking sexy corpse. Some real knockout tits on her." With his index finger, Jacko traced some of the crisscrossing new welts and old bruises that adorned her back and thighs, then laughed out loud. "Dead girl was a freak for sure when she still had blood in her."

Thugg wasn't interested. He shook his head at the other young man. Sometimes Jacko didn't seem right in the head. Who the hell really wanted to fuck a dead person? But then, despite himself, he felt curious. He walked over to the bed, leaned behind the dead girl, and slit the cords binding her wrists and ankles. He stepped away as she sprawled freely on the bed with her buttocks raised.

"Alright, dude," he told Jacko, "go for it."

After pouring the blood in the bucket into the plastic can, Thugg sat and watched Jacko fuck the dead girl. At first he was amused at the contrast between the copulating pair—Jacko's grunts and exertions and the seriousness on his face and how his hard penis stabbed deeper and deeper into the girl's body, while she just lay there limp and used up with her eyes open, looking perplexed but at the same time eerily at peace with herself and the world.

But then Jacko thrust really deep into the dead girl and she shit herself in a long creamy stream that completely browned up his pubic hair, and Thugg decided "Fuck it" and walked over to stare out of the clubroom window instead, at the street and the cars passing by the D.O.A clubhouse building.

Behind him he heard Jacko grunt faster and faster and the slapping together of the two bodies becoming more rapid until Jacko groaned really loudly.

There was a pause, and then Jacko gasped: "Damn, Thugg bro, it was better than I thought. You sure you don't wanna fuck her too?"

Thugg turned around then and stared knives at him. "Hell no, man, I'm sure as hell I fucking don't." Then he calmed and laughed to put everything in its proper perspective. "You know you're weird, man? Really frigging weird?"

Jacko laughed. "Dude, screwing a dead chick is a once-in-a-lifetime experience—I can't go around killing chicks just to hump their corpses, can I? And I don't work for an undertaker? I'm telling ya though, it was worth it; if you don't mind being pooped on." Still laughing, he got up off the dead girl and strode off to light himself a joint and wipe her mess off his crotch and thighs.

Thugg watched him for a moment. *Yeah, that guy's weird alright. He ain't okay in the head at all.*

But then Thugg put things in perspective again: *And Jane is weird in her own way too. That lady is even freakier than Jacko.* He repressed an involuntary shudder. *What the hell does Jane want the dead girl's blood for? Is she gonna cast spells with it?*

In the end, it didn't matter. What mattered was that they'd earned some money, and he could take his new girl Cindy out partying tonight, have a great dinner with her and some sweaty sex later. Jacko could keep his necrophilia; Thugg liked living girls.

But first . . .

Thugg got out his knife again. Now that Jacko was finished, he had to cut out something that Jane wanted from the dead girl's body.

Something that made even less sense than delivering her half a gallon of the girl's blood.

CHAPTER 29

Jane

At about 7 p.m. that evening, an hour before Scott and Caitlin were due over for dinner, Jane heard her front door buzzer ring.

She answered the door. It was the D.O.A leader, Thugg, bringing her the red plastic can of blood and small wrapped package that she'd requested.

She invited him in, but he was in a hurry, said he had a date.

She was too busy herself to insist, so she just kissed him sweetly on the lips and sent him on his way. She'd already paid him.

Once Thugg had walked out of her driveway, Jane carried the blood-can and package down to her basement. She put the blood in one of the freezers.

Jane had often considered saving her menses and making menstrual blood sausages from it. The problem was that she'd not yet found a way to collect enough blood. Even if she froze her menses, it would take forever to get enough to use.

So she'd decided on another approach—using someone else's blood for her blood sausages. Not one of her 'surgery' patients, but someone she couldn't afford to leave alive.

Someone like Ghost. She guessed Ghost really was a ghost now.

Jane giggled. She wasn't in the least bit superstitious. The girl's death was regrettable. *But . . . I really can't leave alive anyone who can identify me.*

At least she was putting the dead girl to good use. The amount of blood Thugg had brought over would be more than sufficient for her blood sausage recipe and . . .

The second package excited her even more. She smiled as she unwrapped it.

If Jane couldn't have menstrual blood sausage, she'd figured she could at least have the next best thing: womb wieners and burgers— her own special recipe, courtesy of the young lady named Ghost.

She finished opening the package. Her smile broadened as she stared at the gory collection of meat arranged on the basement table.

Thugg had cut out Ghost's entire vagina and womb for her. Complete with her labia and clitoris. And the ovaries too, for that distinctive, unbeatable estrogen-loaded feminine taste that men love. (Before sending Thugg off to do her killing for her, Jane had drawn a clear diagram of a woman's lower insides for him and explained exactly which parts of Ghost she wanted delivered.)

Down there in her basement, Jane wasted no time in grinding up Ghost's sexual organs and seasoning them. Then she put the spicy minced mix in the same freezer as the blood, ready for packing into sausage casings.

She'd make hot dogs from it for Scott and herself. Maybe for Caitlin too. *Scotty's right—I'd best start being a good prospective stepmother to his daughter. And hosting her birthday dinner tonight is a step in the right direction.*

While leaving her basement, Jane stared back at her freezers one last time.

She laughed: "See, Ghost?—I wasn't lying, I really am going to eat your tight little pussy."

CHAPTER 30

Caitlin

That same night, Caitlin Hamilton woke up at 2 a.m. to the scared feeling that she wasn't alone in her bedroom.

Then she remembered she wasn't actually in her bedroom. She was upstairs in Jane's house, in the guest bedroom.

The birthday dinner had been a roaring success. Which of course meant that all three of them had drunk too much, and that later on, neither she nor her father had been in any condition to drive them home.

Her father was next door with Jane. Earlier, before dropping off to sleep, Caitlin had thought she'd heard bed noises and female moans.

I guess they weren't that drunk, she'd thought.

And now she found herself awake again and inexplicably frightened.

What woke me? she wondered. Except for a shaft of moonlight coming from the open window and forming a square on the opposite wall, the room was in darkness.

But then something moved out of that darkness onto the moonlit patch of wall. 'Moved onto,' because all it was was a shadow.

Now that Caitlin's eyes had adjusted to the darkness, she saw clearly that she *was* alone in the bedroom. So there was nothing in the room making the shadow. Unless it was standing outside the house and blocking off the moonlight.

But that too was impossible: *I'm up on the second floor.*

The shadow gained more definition. It was still faint, but its edges became less fuzzy.

Now Caitlin felt even more scared. She was staring at a silhouette of a rabbit's head, a rabbit with really large ears, and with massive clunky feet that extended well behind its body.

But then the rabbit shadow turned towards her and she saw that it didn't have large feet at all. She seemed instead to be staring at a rabbit's head on a human body.

And now, listening over the sound of her heart's pounding and the wind that had suddenly begun blowing outside the bedroom, Caitlin thought she heard a soft voice coming from the rabbit-shadow.

"Jane," it whispered. "Jane! Jane!"

Caitlin lay there with the duvet clutched tightly to her breasts, trying not to scream.

Even after the shadow stopped speaking and moved off the wall, Caitlin remained terrified.

This is the second time this has happened to me in this house, she worried. *The first time was while I was using the toilet downstairs. What is going on here? What exactly?*

CHAPTER 31

The Urban Legend Investigation People

"It's been two days now since Ghost vanished," Ninja said. "In that time I've made some really worrying discoveries that warranted me calling this emergency meeting."

The other four members of The Urban Legend Investigation People present gave various signs of assent. Miss Media, Playboy, Warrior, Avatar. This time they were meeting in Ninja's place, which looked more like a computer repair shop that someone's residence. The fat man had two couches they could all fit on and a coffee table for their drinks—everywhere else was taken up by laptops, desktop machines, server towers, monitors of various shapes and sizes, twin air conditioning units to cool everything, and a mindboggling array of cables running everywhere and linking things up.

Warrior smiled coldly. "I sense the danger has come to us already," he said.

"Let's hope it hasn't exactly come to that," Miss Media said. She turned to their obese host. "Though I'm curious too, Ninja. You refused to discuss anything either online or on the phone. So what's this about?"

Ninja cleared a pile of DVD recorders off of a chair and pulled the chair up to the couches. He sat. "I think we've found Insane Jane," he said.

"Huh?" This came from Avatar. "Are you sure, man?"

"Yeah, are you certain?" Miss Media seconded, looking cute but powerful in her cream-colored pantsuit which suggested she'd come here directly from her job at Boston City Hall.

Ninja shrugged. "Quite certain. Let me run everything by you guys and let you judge."

"Hey, man, first of all, what are we gonna do about Ghost's disappearance?" Warrior asked. "Even though I dig the thrill of danger, finding Ghost is way more important than apprehending Ms. Cannibal Holocaust. As the spooky lady's compadres, we owe it to her."

"We think Insane Jane may have Ghost," Playboy said, his handsome face creasing in worry. "Ninja thinks her vanishing isn't a coincidence."

"Yes, I'm afraid so," Ninja agreed.

"What?" Avatar and Miss Media both said at the same time. "But how the hell is that possible?" Miss Media then asked. "We've hardly begun searching for her yet."

Ninja shrugged his heavy shoulders at them all and stroked his black mustache. When he spoke his voice was solemn, heavy with the burden of discovery: "It's all just a fucked-up coincidence. Alright, here's what happened: About a week ago, Ghost sent me a search request—just a name and a MasterCard number, and a description of the woman. The woman's name was Lara Hutch. Someone had hired Ghost to find her, but you guys all know she isn't a hacker, so she passed the search on to me." He leaned forward in his chair as if to emphasize his words or make them marginally louder. "Well, I found Lara Hutch's home address and phone number and sent the info back to Ghost. Well, the next day, Ghost and I chatted about another search she was doing—some BDSM porno flick from the eighties that someone wanted. Afterwards I asked her about the previous day's search. It struck me as odd, you know? I mean, who the fuck knows a person's name and credit card number, but doesn't know where they live?"

"What did she say?" Avatar asked.

"She didn't know either. She said it was for a woman named Anna Jeisen that she knew on OTTmeet, and who she wanted to get into bed with." He paused, sipped from a mug of coffee, then added: "For those of you that don't know—meaning of course, Warrior and Avatar—OTTmeet is a sex and dating website, caters to all kinds of freaky tastes. . . . Anyhow, this Anna Jeisen woman was being coy, but she'd promised Ghost that if she got her this particular info on Lara Hutch, she'd hook up with her." He shrugged. "Well, I let it go at that. It wasn't really important, ya know? I thought it might just be a case of a spurned lover . . . well, whatever. Anyhow, I forgot about it until after Ghost went missing."

"She wasn't replying either her emails or texts or answering the phone," Playboy added. "So we knew there was a problem. And when I called the super at her apartment building, he said she'd left home two days ago and hadn't been back since. He also said she'd been dressed up rather funny when she left. 'She looked like a hooker, like she was on her way to solicit someone for sex,' were his exact words. Which struck me as meaning that Ghost had gone for her hookup with Anna Jeisen, but something had gone wrong there."

"How do you spell 'Jeisen'?" Miss Media asked.

Playboy looked at her oddly for a moment, then replied: "J . . . E . . . I . . . S . . . E . . . N."

Playboy fell silent. Ninja took over the narrative again: "So, with alarm bells now ringing loudly in my head, I did some checking up on this Anna Jeisen lady. And I found out two things: First I hacked into OTTmeet and checked their member's records. She'd registered as Anna Jeisen there but I tracked her email account. I discovered Anna Jeisen's real name is Jane Winters, and that she lives here in Worcester."

"And the second thing?" Miss Media asked. She had a strained look on her face now as if her brain had just kicked into turbo mode.

Ninja winced. "You may or may not have caught this on the news—I know I didn't. Lara Hutch is currently in the Saint Vincent Hospital ICU. Three or four nights ago someone visited her at home and sliced off both of her breasts and all the skin on her belly."

"What?"

"These are from the Worcester Police Department files." Ninja pointed a remote control at the giant monitor opposite him, which hung on the wall in the space between the farther ends of the couches. The screen flared to life, revealing a picture of a bandaged-up woman in a hospital bed with a breathing tube in her mouth and life-support machines all around her. The picture then shifted to another image, of the same woman, but naked and blood-spattered, lying in a bed with seemingly the entire front of her body peeled away.

"Ugh!" Miss Media's face twisted up like she'd vomit. "She looks like someone drove a combine harvester over her."

"Fuck!" Avatar yelped.

Indeed, Warrior was the only one smiling now. The three other men's faces were pallid to varying degrees, including that of Ninja who was relaying the news to them.

Ninja turned off the monitor again. "It's not an image I enjoy staring at," he explained.

"I caught that on the radio," Warrior admitted. "I just didn't link it with our investigation."

"So," Ninja finished quietly, "I think we—I mean Ghost—found Insane Jane."

"We can't really be sure of that," Avatar said nervously. "It could be coincidence. You know—"

Warrior erupted into laughter. "Coincidence? C'mon, man, don't joke here. That's *her* Ninja's found. I'm sure of it." Grinning, he rubbed his hands together gleefully, then pulled out his gun. "Now it's time to hunt the bitch down; it sure is."

"I'd like more confirmation," Avatar insisted.

Ninja looked at Playboy, who rolled his eyes. "You heard the man. He's scared, and I assure you I am too."

"Fuck fear. Just confirm it," Avatar said, his eyes narrowing to slits.

"*I'll* confirm it for you," Miss Media told him, leaning forward on the couch. "While Ninja was filling us in, I've been pondering on the name Anna Jeisen. That's why I asked Playboy how it's spelt. See, it struck me right off that there was something contrived about it."

Playboy nodded. "Yeah, it sounds like an energy drink—Annergizing."

"More like a painkiller—Annagesic," Warrior said with a soft laugh.

"Ha ha," Avatar said coldly, then looked curiously at Miss Media. "And, what's your discovery?"

"Well, it's *not* a real name at all. It's an anagram."

"What's an anagram?" Warrior asked. "Remind me, Media lady."

"An anagram is a word or phrase made by rearranging the letters of another word or phrase. That's what Ghost's crush has done. She just rearranged something else to make herself a screen name."

"Yeah?" Avatar looked unconvinced.

Miss Media nodded. "Oh yes." She peered intently around at them all. "Anna Jeisen is an anagram of Insane Jane."

Ninja looking stunned. "You're sure of this?"

Miss Media nodded. "It's not a mere coincidence. The letters are all complete." She settled back on the couch again, then shrugged. "So there you have it, guys. *She is* Insane Jane."

"Damn," Warrior said with an admiring laugh. "I'd never have guessed that in a hundred years. The cannibal bitch has been fooling us all from the beginning."

Everyone else just looked confounded. The room was silent except for the ambient clicks and hums of Ninja's digital appliances.

After a while, Avatar asked, "So what now? Do we hand her over to the cops?"

Warrior scowled. "C'mon, dude, don't be a spoilsport."

Avatar scowled back. "One of us is likely already dead because of this crazy woman."

"Guys, guys," Ninja said with a placatory raising of his hands. "We can't involve the police in this." He grinned fatly, gesturing around the room at the server towers with their banks of flickering lights. "If we do, I'll most likely go to jail for a long time for a lot of things."

"So what then?" Avatar asked again. "We can't let her get away with it."

"Well," Ninja said, "we have the drop on this lady. She has no idea that we know who she is. We can still catch her."

"She may have tortured Ghost and found out about us," Playboy pointed out.

Miss Media got up and paced the little available space between the couch she'd been sitting on and the television next to it. Her words came out worried: "Why should Insane Jane torture Ghost, except for maybe the sheer pleasure of doing so? She has no reason to question Ghost about our activities, simply because she doesn't know we exist. And Ghost wouldn't volunteer that info either; she's most likely keeping mum, waiting for us to rescue her."

"No," Warrior said with finality. "Ghost is dead."

"How can you be certain of that?" Miss Media asked, fear showing on her face. "I believe she's waiting for us to rescue her."

Warrior shook his head. "Trust me on this—Ghost is deader than the sand outside of this apartment building. You can almost expect her to start haunting us." He smirked. "Our target won't keep Ghost alive; it'd be too dangerous to do."

Playboy put down his beer and nodded. "I agree. It's either that, or the pair of them are having the longest lesbian sex session in history, with Guinness World Records recording."

Ninja got to his feet; upright, the big man was an impressive sight. "Lady and gentlemen, let's not distract ourselves. Like it or not, our course has been decided for us. We've found Insane Jane; and we now owe it both to ourselves and to Ghost's memory to take the woman down."

"Yeah, I say we hunt the bitch down," Warrior instantly agreed. He looked around at the others. "What do you guys say?"

Playboy frowned. "Well, that was the plan from the beginning, wasn't it?"

Warrior looked at their sole female companion. "Media?"

She stopped pacing; sat back down. "Oh, alright, I'm in."

Warrior gave Avatar a hard look. "Dude, time to put up or shut up. Which is it?"

Avatar smirked back at him. "I ain't yellow, man. I'm just more cautious than you. I gotta be: I'm too thin to lose any meat off my bones."

There was strained laughter all around.

"Which is it then?" Warrior asked when the laughter had subsided.

"I'm with you guys. Let's hunt her down. Make Ghost proud of us."

That settled, Warrior turned back to Ninja. "So, oh wise man of the world-wide computers, now we know who Jane is and *where* she is. That's a good start. But tell us. . . what more do the urban legends say about her?"

"Yeah," Avatar seconded, "something to give us an edge. She's clearly smarter than a fox—not to mention a whole lot deadlier—and we can't just walk up to her on the street and grab her."

"Do you have any pictures of her?" Miss Media added. "What the hell does she look like?"

Ninja swept a moody gaze over them all. "One thing at a time, Media. Yes, I do have a couple of snaps on my hard drive. But first, let's discuss Warrior's question . . ."

He focused his full attention on the little man in black leather who now had eagerness written all over his hard face. "Well, dude, according to several accounts, Insane Jane is utterly terrified of mirrors . . ."

PART 3: IN THE END, THE THINGS YOU DO AND DO WILL FINALLY DO YOU TOO

CHAPTER 32

Jane In The Past – 3

The little girl's eyes widened as she watched Mr. Floppyears pull off the front passenger door of her parents' burning car.

"No! Stop!" she yelled after him. "Come back! You'll die too!"

She was certain of this. Both of her parents and her little brother were already dead, burnt up in the car.

But the rabbit-headed man didn't pay her any attention.

Jane looked off down the road, to where the blue pickup truck that had hit them lay upside down, with its wheels still spinning as if it was driving on the air. All its windows were shattered and she could see a man hanging limp in the driver's seat—upside-down like his vehicle. She thought she saw blood dripping from the man's upside-down head.

A loud noise distracted her, forced her attention back to herself and the road again.

Her parents' car had just exploded. The last thing she saw as the fire spurted sky-high was Mr. Floppyears being blown backwards towards her, then she covered her eyes with her little hands.

After a while she peeked through her fingers. The explosion was over, so she put her hands down again.

All at once young Jane was struck by the change in her surroundings:

This was somewhere different. She was still sitting against a roadside tree, but now the tree was a blackened rotting husk. The ground under her was no longer grassy, but hot black stone. As though frozen in permanent dusk, the sky was dark with orange streaks in it. It looked like she was viewing strips of the sun sliced by dark shutters.

The car she'd been in was now a charred, tireless and door-less framework.

Fire was burning all around the car. Fire was burning everywhere the little girl looked. Not big fires—just lots of little fires which spurted up from cracks in the ground; orange and yellow spurts.

None of the flames came anywhere near little Jane. She sat there beneath her strange withered tree and looked around. In the distance were lots of similarly withered trees. A short distance away, the truck that had caused the accident was still upside-down, but now there was a fleshless skeleton strapped upside-down in the driver's seat. And the truck no longer had any tires, but the tire rims were still spinning as if the skeleton was driving somewhere in the sky.

Then she saw that Mr. Floppyears was walking towards her. He was unharmed.

Jane was relieved that her new friend hadn't died when her parents' car exploded. If he had, she had no idea what she'd have done. It was bad enough that she was confused now, but at least she had an adult friend—adults were great to have around when children were confused.

Mr. Floppyears was dragging something behind him. She stared at the thing and felt very scared. He was dragging her father's burnt corpse. (She knew it was her father's corpse because it was too big to be her mother's.) As Mr. Floppyears pulled the corpse towards her, it bounced on the warm stones and snagged on rocks, and when it did so, little charred bits of it chipped off. Father's body was all bent and twisted now, just like how birds looked when they died. His clothes were all burnt away; he was just a bare, blackened and smoking mess.

Once again, little Jane was too surprised to cry.

"What do you want with my daddy?" she asked Mr. Floppyears.

"Oh, I thought you must be hungry by now," he replied.

Jane thought this was an odd reply, simply because her father, being dead, couldn't buy treats for her anymore like he always did. She was about to point this out to Mr. Floppyears when she realized that he looked somehow different now.

Yes, the rabbit-headed man *was* different. First of all, he now had two curling ram's horns sticking out of his forehead. And secondly, his teeth, which had originally been long blunt bunny teeth, now looked like those of a wolf. Still long, but scary-long now.

"So, are you hungry, Jane?" he asked nicely.

She thought about it and nodded, though there wasn't anything anywhere around to eat. They were now in the middle of nowhere, without a shop in sight. Nothing to see but the flames spurting up from the rocky ground and the wasted and crazily twisted trees scattered everywhere. So where could they buy hot dogs or candy bars or ice cream?

But now too, she suddenly felt more hungry than she had in a long time.

In fact, Jane doubted if she'd ever felt this hungry before in her life.

"Let's eat then," Mr. Floppyears said nicely. Then he bent and broke off one of Father's burnt legs. After scraping the charred skin off its thigh, he ripped off some of its roasted flesh and held it out to Jane. "Try it, little girl—you'll like it."

The little girl hesitated. True, the part of Father that Mr. Floppyears was offering her smelled delicious—she was already salivating fiercely, the drool dribbling all over her chin and down onto her dress—but wasn't it wrong to eat other people? And particularly, one's own daddy?

"Don't be afraid, Jane," Mr. Floppyears urged. "Go on. Look, I'm going to eat some of your daddy too." And with that, he popped a chunk of Father's leg into his mouth and chewed happily. Then he ate some more. Jane saw that his hands had altered too—now they looked like lizard's feet with long black nails.

Still, she didn't feel scared of him at all.

Little Jane was so hungry. She did what Mr. Floppyears was doing and ate some of her father as well. She was glad she did. Father tasted as delicious as he smelled.

They sat there under the strangely blighted tree, staring at the heat-blasted landscape and the two burnt-out vehicles, and eating, chewing blithely away, until after a while Jane felt really full and tired and fell asleep.

As she fell asleep, Jane felt Mr. Floppyears stroking her hair and saying:

"Now, little girl, go out into the big wide world and eat a lot more human meat. I'll be with you. I'll be watching over you, little Jane."

"Okay," she replied drowsily.

CHAPTER 33

Jane

Jane woke up.

Damn, I dreamt of Mr. Floppyears again. Why the hell won't he simply let me be? Not being able to use mirrors is one thing, but him haunting my dreams is altogether too much. Oh, how I wish I could visit a shrink!

It was morning; daylight was streaming in through her bedroom drapes.

Jane got up and got ready for work.

***

For a while now, Jane had been pondering a dilemma: *do I love Scotty or not?*

Walking to work this Thursday morning in late August, with the suggestion of autumn already in the air, keeping her eyes low so she didn't look at any reflective storefront windows, the same question filled her mind:

Do I love Scotty or don't I?

Jane's consideration of this problem was a reversal of most other women's thinking. To Jane, true love was dangerous and something to be avoided at all costs. True love would weaken her. It would slacken her resolve to be who she needed to be.

She felt it would make her less efficient in fulfilling her life's purpose.

I'm safe with Scotty if I don't love him. But if I do . . . I'll have to either leave him or kill him. Yes, then I'll have to kill him. And that'll be a real shame because I like him so much.

Now that Jane had met Scott's daughter Caitlin, the situation had grown even more complicated. She liked how she and Caitlin got along well with each other, but that just meant that sooner or later, Scott would be proposing to her. Here too, something that would make most women in a relationship happy, if only because it proved the man's commitment, was a source of potential distress to Jane.

She arrived at Cashstretch without staring into any windows. She changed into her blue and orange uniform, clipped on her name tag, then took her place at Checkout Counter 4 and began attending to the day's army of shoppers. Cereal, drinks, frozen foods, baby things, menswear and womenswear; toys, toys and more toys; cosmetics and perfumes, pet foods, cans of conceivably everything that could be canned, media players and the CDs and DVDs to power them, pastries and sausages and assorted butters and cheeses, house decorations and kitchenware, organic fruits, free-range and caged-hen eggs, cellphones and earphones, paperbacks and stationary, toiletries . . . these varied purchases all flashed before her and around her (Danielle was on her immediate left and José on her right) in the course of the next three hours, becoming the indisputable facts of her existence.

In the mental spaces between clients, the question still hung in Jane's mind though: *Do I love Scotty or don't I? Yes, in my heart of hearts I do have sweet and tender feelings for him, but are they now rooted deep enough to endanger me? I really don't want to hurt Scotty, but I may need to, to protect myself from myself . . . I can just pay Thugg to dispose of his body afterwards.*

Outwardly, Jane smiled at customer after customer, scanned their purchases and accepted their payments, but inwardly, she felt immensely distressed.

She was still pondering the state of her romantic life when the good-looking couple walked in through the store's front entrance.

Jane's thoughts immediately switched from her boyfriend to the pair: *Wow, they're perfect. They're both absolutely perfect!*

CHAPTER 34

Playboy, Miss Media, Jane

Playboy and Miss Media studied Jane too. They already knew which of the Cashstretch cashiers she was from the pictures Ninja had shown them.

"That's her?" Playboy asked in a low voice. "She looks so normal, I feel disappointed. In those photos she seemed exotic and exciting."

Miss Media made her own visual appraisal of the woman currently manning Counter 4. A pretty redhead with a welcoming smile. "You wouldn't like to date her then? Dude, you date just about anyone else in a skirt."

"Nope. She'll likely bite off my dick," he whispered back to her.

"Okay," Miss Media said, "remember Ninja's instructions: Now that we know she's here, we don't look at her. We don't give her any reason to suspect we're here because of her."

"Yeah." Arm in arm, they strolled over to where the shopping carts were parked and got one each.

Miss Media smiled sweetly at Playboy. "So, darling, what exactly are we buying in this place?"

***

Ninja's plan was dangerous but deviously simple:

"There's only one surefire way to trap Insane Jane," he'd said. "We'll entice her with live bait." Then he'd looked around the meeting and pointed at Playboy and Miss Media. "Which means you two." He'd raised a fat hand to stifle Miss Media's protests. "Sorry, baby, but you and my cousin are the fittest and best-looking of all of us here." He indicated his own corpulent bulk. "I guess we've finally discovered a disadvantage to spending time in the gym."

Avatar, Warrior, and another female TULIP member who'd arrived later—Rosebud—had laughed at that.

"I don't like it," Miss Media had complained. "Hey—why can't Warrior and Avatar go? Or Rosie instead of me?"

Ninja had rolled his eyes and made a wide, encompassing gesture with his hands. "Because . . . now let me see . . ." He tapped the air with a finger. "Oh yeah, it's like this: Warrior's uglier than Satan himself, Avatar has no meat on his body to interest our cannibal damsel, and Rosie's a card-carrying pussy—in a non-sexual way, of course: she's scared of the sight of her own pee, not to mention her menses. All our quarry has to do is frown at her and she'll blabber out the whole plan."

Warrior grinned at the remark; Avatar shrugged; Rosebud looked embarrassed.

"So now that that's settled," Ninja went on, "here's what we'll do: You two dress up to show off your bodies—imagine you're meat in a butcher's window—you gotta wear sporty clothes like you're coming from or heading for a workout—shorts, muscle shirts, sneakers. Hey, Media, wear flip-flops to show off those toned ankles of yours. You never know—the lady might want to eat some big toes too."

"Screw you, man!"

Ninja raised his hands in mock surrender. "Hey, hey, don't shoot the messenger—you know we do whatever it takes. You gotta let our girl see *all* the goods. Hopefully she'll bite."

Miss Media had frowned at that. "Bite, huh? You're sure you ain't just dispatching us to get eaten?"

Ninja had grinned back. "Don't take it personal, babe. We'll be there to ensure *that* doesn't happen."

And that had been that. It had taken them just three days to work out their plan and get things properly set up. Where to set their trap? Playboy owned an isolated cottage on the north side of Worcester that he sometimes used as a love nest and which TULIP occasionally used as their HQ. Everything else was just a question of logistics.

The final piece of the puzzle that needed fitting was knowing the earliest day off Miss Media could get from work.

Which had been Thursday.

And so today Thursday, Playboy and Miss Media had dressed up in sporty clothes and headed for Cashstretch, posing as a married couple.

***

"Damn, but she really does seem so *normal*, you know," Miss Media whispered back to Playboy as they joined the queue in front of Jane's checkout counter. "And she's so pretty too; her red hair is like sunset, and her green eyes look like traffic lights."

Miss Media smiled to quell her nervousness. It wasn't that she lacked courage, just that the memory of Ghost's fate haunted her. She whispered back to Playboy again: "Dude, I can seriously imagine you taking her out for dinner at the Hilton, and you both doing some bed-wrestling afterwards."

Playboy turned from staring at Counter 3, where the attendant, 'Danielle' by her name tag, looked both very bored and very pregnant. "Uh uh, count me out," he whispered. "Dinner with this chick would more likely be at the *Kil*ton, with me on the menu and Jeffrey Dahmer as her date."

The customer currently at the counter wheeled away her bags of frozen lasagna and yoghurts, adult diapers, bread, sardines, and foot-long sausages. Next in line was a blond kid with a skateboard who was buying some CDs. And then it was their turn.

***

Jane smiled at the married couple. They were both young and very good-looking. The dark-haired husband was large and well-sculpted. The blonde wife was less muscular but had clearly also done her share of hard time in the gym. They seemed quite wealthy too.

They seem a little ill at ease, as if they had a fight while walking the shopping aisles.

Watching them from the corner of her eye while attending to the skateboard boy in front of them, Jane had already made up her mind on which portions of each she wanted. For the husband, it had to be his pecs. That broad chest would look so great in her freezer. She could already taste the sizzling steaks she'd make from it. And maybe one of his biceps also. Muscular arms like this guy had could either be wrapped around you while making love, or stewed in a pot.

The wife had great hips and thighs. *So, that's her loss then—both thighs. I might take her right buttock too, just in case I like the taste of her better that I do him. It isn't like I can go back for second helpings.*

That decided, Jane put on her nicest demeanor and attended to the pair, who were buying mostly home décor stuff—two framed paintings, a couple of duvets, a set of throw pillow covers, two vases, a jar of potpourri—and a pair of skis:

"So that'll be $189, sir. . . . Sir, ma'am, I'm delighted to inform you that you qualify for our Bahamas Cruise competition . . . please just fill out this form, with your name, address and telephone number . . ."

There was a slight hiccup then. The husband looked at the wife. "Honey, do you think we should bother? Remember we're jetting off to Switzerland on Monday."

"Yes, let's enter, dear." The blonde wife took the blue card from Jane and studied it. "Oh, we'll only be gone for two months anyway. We'll be back before the winners are announced." She simpered at her man and pouted a red lipstick 'O.' "Please, baby, I really wanna go down south." Then she straightaway looked embarrassed, stared at Jane, and giggled. "Oh, I'm sorry, I don't mean it like that. I mean . . . you know . . ."

Jane instantly wrote the wife off as another trophy airhead. The woman fit the 'dumb blonde' stereotype to a 'T.'

The husband filled in the contest form. Jane memorized the details. The man's credit card had already identified him as Dominic Taylor. She now knew that the wife was called Jane too (what a coincidence, though definitely not in the intelligence department) and that they lived in Burncoat, at the upper limits of the city.

She handed the card back to the man, indicated where he should drop it off, and wished them both a nice day. She interpreted the husband's backward glances at her as he wheeled his cart towards the front entrance as sexual desire.

I'm not into threesomes, asshole. Stick it in your airhead.

***

Outside, Miss Media felt relieved.

"I've never felt so spooked in my life," she told Playboy as they loaded what they'd bought into the trunk of his white Nissan SUV.

"When she was looking at us, it felt like her eyes were scalpels peeling the meat from my bones."

"I still find it hard to accept that she's the one though," Playboy said, glancing back at the Cashstretch entrance. "Yeah, we know that she is, but even after meeting her in person, it's hard to believe."

"It's her normalcy trick. I'm sure even your boy Jeff Dahmer seemed to be just a regular guy till that handcuffed guy escaped from his apartment."

They got into the SUV and drove off.

"Well, she has our home address on that form," Playboy said as he turned out of the parking lot onto Main Street. "Now all we gotta do is wait for her to bite the bait."

"*I'm* the bait. I'm not waiting to get bit."

"You're so touchy, Media. It's just a figure of speech."

***

Jane now found herself faced with a crisis.

While attending to the next customers, she pondered what to do. If she did this 'surgery,' it would be her fourth in three months.

Maybe I should put it off. I've more than enough meat at home. But they'll be travelling in four days time. Of course they'll be back, but . . . NO!

She felt a strong urging towards visiting Dominic and Jane Taylor—her view of the woman's buttocks as she'd strode towards the front entrance had been very compelling. That ass was superb, lean meat with very little fat. The tantalizing sight had instantly made her reverse her selection from 'thighs' to 'ass.'

Jane Winters had almost enough human flesh at home to make up a complete person, but she didn't have any buttocks. So Jane Taylor's ass called to her as loudly as if it had a megaphone pressed to its anus.

I must have that ass in my freezer. I don't want her going and killing herself in the Alps on some airhead skiing pursuit and robbing me of it. I'm going to have to visit them before they leave for their vacation.

That decided, Jane began to plot and scheme: *Hmm, if Monday's their travel date, Saturday night's my best bet. But first things first. I'll drive out there tonight for a look-see . . .*

CHAPTER 35

The Urban Legend Investigation People

About 1 a.m. the next morning.

Warrior scratched the stubble on his chin. "Well, the hungry bitch sure did bite the doggie bone," he said, gesturing at the monitor before him, at the woman climbing out of the black van that had parked a short distance down Burncoat Street two minutes earlier.

Warrior was seated beside Miss Media in the rear of the TULIP surveillance van. The large white van, which was parked in Playboy's driveway, would appear empty to any observers, locked and with all its lights off. But its rear was full of monitors and communication equipment.

The house itself—they'd chosen Playboy's weekend love nest for their trap because of its isolation—seemed asleep for the night. Its exterior lights were on, the interior ones off.

Miss Media flicked a switch, then spoke briskly into her headphone mic. "Guys, she's here."

"Okay, we're waiting," came back Ninja's voice. "Keep us posted on which entrance she's using."

"You did leave them *all* open, didn't you?"

"Yeah. She'll find it easier to get inside than peeing. Avatar is rechecking the back door now."

Warrior spoke into his own microphone: "Is everyone in position?"

"Yeah, I'm out front in the living room. Playboy is in bed. I think he's really asleep. Though how anyone can sleep at a time like this beats me."

"Okay, we'll keep you posted," Miss Media said. "Insane Jane is on her way over to the house now. Once she's inside we'll come join you guys." She cut the connection and turned to stare at the main monitor.

The high-definition night-vision cameras she'd earlier mounted on the trees around Playboy's cottage brought her four different views of the approaching woman. Yes, it was the same pretty lady from the supermarket, though on the huge screen with its alien-green colors, she looked like someone in a found-footage movie: her red hair now looked black, while her green eyes were ghost circles. She had on a dark jumpsuit with the hoodie down and sneakers.

"Something's wrong," Warrior said.

"How d'you mean?" Miss Media asked him.

Warrior laughed and slapped his knee. "Yeah, this lady ain't no fool, that's for sure."

Miss Media swiveled her seat to stare at him. "Explain yourself."

He in turn pointed to the screen. "Look at her hands. She's only carrying a set of binoculars. That means she's here just for surveillance. Just to have a look around. She wants to make sure she can get into the house without any hitches." He stroked his chin. "It's a fifty-to-one wager that all her surgical equipment is back at home."

Miss Media returned her attention to the screen. Now she noticed the binoculars Jane was carrying.

"Looks like you're right," she agreed with Warrior. "What do we do now?"

"Turn on my mic."

She flicked a switch. Warrior spoke into his microphone: "Hey, Ninja, can you hear me?"

"Loud and clear, dude. Go on."

"Alright, she's here, but she's not here for business tonight. You guys lock all the entrances again, except for the kitchen door."

"Hey, you sure 'bout this?"

"Yeah, yeah," Miss Media agreed, not taking her eyes from the green-tinged monitor, on which their quarry could clearly be seen crouching behind a tree and training her binoculars on the house. "I see where Warrior's going with this: If our girl was here to operate, it wouldn't matter how many doors we left open; she'd use the first one she found. But if she goes around the house checking the locks tonight and finds all the doors are open, it's gonna look suspicious to her. Remember she's very smart."

"What if you two are wrong?"

"We aren't wrong—she's not carrying her knives. She'll be back for sure."

"Okay, we'll get on it."

Miss Media cut the connection. Warrior looked at her, then gestured to his bag of weapons, which sat on a vacant chair in the surveillance van. "But, what if we're both wrong and she *doesn't* return? How 'bout if I just sneak out there and neutralize her right now? I can have her tied up in a jiffy."

Miss Media shook her head at him. "C'mon, man, you know that's not what this is about. Yes, she's a danger to society, but she's also a fascinating urban legend, and we need *proof* that she's who she is—so we'll wait for her return."

"What if she doesn't return?"

Miss Media tapped the screen and shivered. "Oh, she'll be back, alright. She most definitely will. You need to have seen the way she was looking at Playboy and I in the supermarket. Like she couldn't wait to sink her teeth into our bodies."

"Hmmm, interesting." Warrior resumed scratching his chin as they watched Jane stealthily cross the front yard toward the cottage and begin checking its doors and windows. "So this means her second visit here is gonna be either tomorrow night or Saturday night. She's unlikely to cut it as close as Sunday." He grinned at Jane's image. "Just come, crazy lady. We'll be here to welcome you."

"I wonder how she gets into houses with security systems?" Miss Media mused.

Warrior shrugged back. "I guess when you're hungry enough, there's always a way to get to your food."

CHAPTER 36

Jane

On Saturday morning, just as Jane was crosschecking her preparations for the night, her cellphone rang.

It was Caitlin. But there was something wrong with the girl. Even before Caitlin had said a word, her sobs had already conveyed her frayed emotional state across the connection.

Jane was bemused. She put down the scalpel she'd been testing for sharpness and asked: "Caitlin, what's wrong?" A worried thought stabbed her breast. "Hey, nothing's happened to Scott, has it?"

Caitlin continued sobbing on the line.

Jane sat down beside her basement worktable and, keeping the phone held to her ear, picked up a cleaver with her free hand. She caught a flash of a reflection in the blade and hastily put it down again. She hated cleavers. With their wide flat blades they were too much like mirrors. It was just that tonight, with two 'patients' to be operated on, she'd occasionally need a blade larger than a scalpel. A long cutting edge that could penetrate deep into the meat of the matter.

Jane glanced at the cleaver. She felt an intense thrill of terror at what she'd almost seen. Because she'd been certain she'd almost seen *him* in there . . .

She rallied her courage; she needed this damn cleaver. *I just have to hold it right, so the blade faces to the sides and not at me! And—*

Meanwhile, Caitlin was still weeping on the phone. Jane put her own thoughts on hold: "Caitlin, what's the matter with you? Please say something, will you? You're making me very worried."

"Please, Jane . . . please, I'm begging you! Please stay away from my dad and me. Please keep away from us!"

Jane was shocked, momentarily thrown off balance. She sat there with the phone at her ear, staring at the array of surgical tools spread out in front of her and pondering Caitlin's words.

Alright, now this is unprecedented for sure.

"Caitlin, what are you talking about? What on earth is going on? Why are you begging me to stay away from your father!?"

She'd put sufficient emotion into her voice that the other young woman felt it across their digital connection.

"Just stay away from us, Jane! Please! Please! Please!"

"But why? Is it something I did or said that upset you?"

"No no no! We both like you. Daddy's in love with you!" More sobbing. "Please, I'm begging you."

"Does Scott know about this?"

No reply; just a whole lot of weeping. And, the way Caitlin was slurring her words a little, it sounded as if she'd been drinking too.

But by now Jane already suspected what the problem might be.

"Okay, let's do it like this," she said, forcing an icy calm upon herself. *This silly girl mustn't ruin my wedding plans.* "Caitlin, I'm really busy at the moment, and I can't talk long on the phone, but I'll meet you for lunch . . . Okay? . . . Yes, then we'll thrash all this nonsense out . . ."

Once Caitlin had agreed to meet up for lunch, Jane hung up and got back to selecting the right scalpel for tonight's job.

After awhile she got up and went upstairs to cut herself a slice of the cake she'd baked using Lara Hutch's belly fat.

CHAPTER 37

Caitlin, mostly . . .

As Caitlin had expected, Jane didn't believe her in the least.

". . . A large bunny-like man in your bedroom, who said he'd kill and eat both you and your father? You're sure you weren't drunk at the time?"

"No, Jane, I wasn't drunk."

Jane peered closely at her across their table. They were seated outside the Corner Grille pizza place up on Pleasant Street, sharing a harvest moon pizza. Both women were drinking iced teas. This afternoon the weather was warm. Sitting outside here gave Jane a great panoramic street view, made her feel like she was right in the middle of life. "Caitlin, you don't do drugs, do you? LSD or other hallucinogenics?"

"No, I don't do drugs, you bitch. Fuck you for saying that!" Caitlin snapped back. "If I knew you'd asked me to lunch just to insult me, I wouldn't have bothered driving out from Boston. I've better ways to waste my time."

The terrifying incident had happened last night and Caitlin was now over her crying fit. If anything, she was now angry at being subjected to this nonsense and very prepared to take out her anger on Jane, whom she viewed as being its direct or indirect cause.

Jane immediately apologized. "I'm sorry, Caitlin. It's just that this whole story of yours lacks credibility. Listen—I love your father with all my heart, and he clearly loves me too; so why should I allow your bad dreams separate us? You've clearly just got an overactive imagination."

"I *did not* imagine it. This is the *third* time it's happened: The first time was in your toilet. Next was the night I stayed over at your place. And now *this*."

Jane scowled. "So, from poop to pillowcases. And now he's visiting you at home?"

"This isn't a joke. Just stay well clear of dad and I. It's our lives that the damn bunny-man is threatening, not yours."

Jane smirked and sipped her iced tea. "But why should I? All you're doing is throwing a tantrum, like a ten-year-old who's scared her father will cease loving her once he remarries."

Caitlin felt like she'd cry at the accusation. "That's not true. I'm not . . ."

Jane glared at her. "Let me finish, you spoilt daddy's-little-girl. You're not throwing a tantrum, honeybunch? Alright then, just listen to yourself: You want me to break off my relationship with your father, because you've been seeing Mr. Floppyears, and he's been threatening to kill your family. Well, that's just selfish. You're being entirely unfair to me and . . ."

Jane said quite a lot more, most of it angry and some of it weepy, but Caitlin didn't interrupt her because she didn't hear any of it. Because, all of a sudden, while Jane was on her emotional rant, her body had seemed to alter, her head changing its shape and size. Her red hair seemed to shorten and turn white, while her ears each appeared to lengthen out to several feet long. Her nose shot forward into an almost rat-like snout with an underside of fat yellow teeth. The image wavered, holding but fading in and out, a semitransparent overlay beneath which a human skull was visible.

Caitlin didn't know what was going on. She didn't know what she was seeing. She looked around. None of the people walking past the pizza parlor had noticed anything amiss.

But then she blinked, and suddenly Jane was perfectly normal again. Jane was also sobbing gently at being so unappreciated.

"And I love him so damn much, and you don't want us to be together," Jane wept. "You're just so selfish, so damn selfish. Just another self-centered daddy's girl."

All Caitlin could think during the rest of their lunch was: *Oh, my God! Oh, my God! She's responsible for the bunny-man tormenting me!* She ate some more of their pizza and drank her iced tea only because she was scared of making Jane angry if she didn't. After that 'flash' vision, Caitlin no longer possessed an appetite.

Jane though, ate as voraciously as ever, as though her adamant passion for Caitlin's father was best expressed by stuffing herself as fast as possible.

They parted at the end of lunch with Caitlin entirely agreeing with Jane's point of view that her relationship with Scott had to continue, hopefully to the marriage altar even, while all the while nearly peeing herself from sheer fright.

Caitlin drove back to Boston in absolute terror, with no idea at all of what to do.

CHAPTER 38

Jane

1:30 a.m.

Jane pulled up beside the same tree as the previous time she'd visited Burncoat Street.

All in all, it had been a good day so far. Her lunch with Caitlin had gone a whole lot better than anticipated. She'd expected Caitlin to stick to her self-centered guns, but . . .

Jane was still rather bemused by Caitlin's sudden about-face.

She changed so abruptly, it was really weird. I'm not that good an actress; all my weeping certainly didn't change her mind. Or did it? But—and once again she felt a heart pang of worry that her feelings for Scott Hamilton had grown too strong—*but I really wasn't acting. At the time I did feel like I was about losing the one man I really need in my life.*

She climbed out of the van and got out her suitcases. *Still, it went well. At least now I don't have to worry about her trying to break us up. Well, I hope I don't. I don't want to have to do something nasty to her. That'd be hitting too close to home.*

She forgot Caitlin. She was here for serious business. She had two people to neutralize, anesthetize, and operate on.

She frowned. Really, one-thirty in the morning was too late for that much cutting. *I have to be away from here by four-thirty, before sunrise. But it can't be helped.*

While making her plans, she'd also figured in some time for the couple to wear themselves out with lovemaking if they were in the mood. This was Saturday night after all.

She hefted her pair of cases, stepped between the trees bordering the road, and sneaked towards the Taylor's cottage. The couple's white SUV was parked out front, meaning they were home.

***

Side of the house. Kitchen door. Same homeowner mistake as last time: once again, the kitchen door left unlocked.

You'd think they'd remember to . . . But then Jane remembered the wife's behavior when the couple had shopped at Cashstretch. *Yes, she's got no brains except in her ass, and I'm here to relieve her of her ass, so she'll shortly have no brains anywhere at all . . . But . . . but even airheads must have some consideration for their personal safety. Or how else do they survive to adulthood?*

Either way it was a moot point. What mattered was that she was inside the house.

As was her usual MO, Jane put down her suitcases in the kitchen, slipped two pre-filled syringes into her pocket, and then walked through the spacious cottage hunting for her prey.

They weren't in their bedroom. She shrugged. Apparently her 'Saturday Night Fucking' theory was right and they'd be asleep in the living room. Just like the Morgan sisters. She hoped that unlike the Morgans, this couple would be through making love now and be fast asleep in one another's arms.

I'll take out the husband first. The wife is certain to be less trouble.

She stepped into the dark living room, instantly making out the pair of bodies lying on the rug, to the left of the nearer of two coffee tables. The living room walls looked oddly reflective in the darkness, but she didn't mind them. She never saw anything in dark mirrors.

Alright, here goes, she thought, flicking on a small penlight and focusing it on the sleeping couple. *Thanks, guys, for making this so easy for all three of us.*

But then, a voice right behind her yelled: "ALRIGHT, NOW!" and suddenly the living room was awash with light.

Jane now discovered that she was surrounded by mirrors. Someone had covered the living room's four walls with mirrors.

***

The 'sleeping' couple on the floor were getting to their feet. Three other people were also stepping into the living room from different angles. None of that bothered Jane—she'd just kill them all.

But what now held Jane transfixed and paralyzed were the images all around her. Her reflections. What she'd avoided looking at for the past twenty years since the car crash that had roasted her parents and brother.

She was surrounded by images of Mr. Floppyears dressed as herself. In the mirrors, at least twenty versions of Mr. Floppyears were silently laughing at her.

Jane began screaming.

"Hey, bitch," someone said, "Ghost sends her regards from the afterlife."

So it was all a trap? Jane understood nothing now. She was too traumatized by the distortions of *herself* all around her. It didn't matter how many photographs of herself she'd seen, didn't matter at all that she knew she was a normal red-blooded human woman like all the others out there; none of that mattered so long as the mirrors showed her a different truth, a corrupted reality she found herself compelled to believe in.

I am Mr. Floppyears and he is Me.

One of the people in the room—a tall bony man—advanced on her with a taser. While still gibbering in horror, Jane reacted on instinct, ducking out of the way of the fired pins so they shattered the mirror behind her, then stepping up close to the man. She punched him in the solar plexus, then as he bent over with his face crumpling up in pain, she hit him a hard chop in the side of the neck. She felt his neck bones shatter . . . he dropped dead.

Jane looked up again, saw Mr. Floppyears clapping his hands in delight all around her, and began screaming again. Now there were tears streaming down her cheeks. She felt like her mind was imploding, like she was going mad . . .

The woman who'd come to Cashstretch was next to attack her. She too had a taser. Jane calculated the trajectory of the taser wires once fired, watched the movement of the woman's trigger finger, and then, in a split-second-timed move she knew she'd find impossible to ever duplicate, she both sidestepped away from the insulated taser wires and grabbed them, while simultaneously spinning round and redirecting the taser needles onto the woman's breasts.

The woman stiffened with the electric shock and dropped. While falling she smacked her head on one of the coffee tables and knocked herself out.

Two down, three to go.

Jane had stopped screaming now. She dared a look into the mirrors. Mr. Floppyears was still in there watching her. Only now, Rabbit-Head wasn't applauding anymore. Now he looked dead serious, like he was willing her on to victory.

Screw you, Floppyears! Jane thought defiantly. *I'll get out of this on my own merits.*

Angry now, she spun around to take the fight to those who'd dared to trap her.

But then something cold and frighteningly painful slammed into her forehead. For a split-second, Jane was aware of her skull exploding with agony, and then she was crashing back onto one of the large couches in the room.

Jane didn't even realize that she was dying. She was surprised, however, to see her life replay in her mind like a movie . . .

CHAPTER 39

Jane in the Past – 4

Of course, the State Police hadn't believed Jane's story. What she'd claimed was impossible: rabbit-headed men didn't rescue young girls from burning cars. The State Police told her she'd hallucinated her rabbit-man. What had happened, they said, was that a 'freak explosion' had blown off the two doors on her side (in her own case, before the car had actually begun burning) and she'd been flung out to safety.

Jane knew better, but after a while she'd realized that no one would believe her and so she'd stopped telling her tale.

It was after that that the thing with the mirrors had started.

***

A mirror isn't innocent, she knew. It's an access road to a parallel universe. We only think that what we're viewing is our exact reflection. But it isn't; even in that familiar self which we see, there are hundreds of little differences from our norm; we don't focus on them simply because they're so minute.

The world of our reflection is a different universe, where we are not the same person we are 'here.'

And if even *we* aren't the same person, who's to say then how much else in there is different?

***

"It's hard to be hard on her," she heard Scott explaining to Caitlin. "Her parents died in an auto crash when she was a kid. She was right there in the car, watched them burn up along with her kid brother."

"Oh my gosh! That happened to her? That's just horrible!"

"I had tears in my eyes too when she told me the story."

***

The bunny-man is my friend. Okay, maybe he doesn't really exist, so then he's my imaginary friend. He has some really weird appetites though . . .

***

Surely, Scott sometimes wondered why she came back horny from work. It was the sight of all that raw meat waltzing back and forth before her. It was so sexy—all that food on display. She however hoped Scott thought it was merely her heartfelt desire for him to penetrate her lady parts that had her so aroused.

***

"Welcome to Cashstretch, sir. Cashstretch: Makes your bottom dollar go much further. . . . Oh, congratulations, sir. You qualify for our Bahamas Cruise competition. . . . Just fill in your name and address right here and . . . and . . . and I'll visit you in a couple of weeks . . ."

***

She remembers:
Sending Ghost old pictures of her Aunt Margaret in place of her own photos.
Aunt Margaret was always very MILF for her age, with those large breasts she'd always been envious of. There had been no chance of her deceit ever being discovered: Aunt Margaret wouldn't be found dead on a site like OTTmeet.

***

Poor Ghost . . . is she waiting for me on the other side of this falling darkness? Those womb wieners did taste delicious though.

***

"A psychopath," Jane heard José Fernández telling Danielle as they finished their shift at the cash registers, "is an individual—either a man or a woman—who sees other human beings as assemblages of separate parts and not as whole persons."

***

Oh, hell no, I'm not crazy! she thought defiantly. *I'm not . . . . not . . . n-n-n . . .*

***

Blackout. And then there was . . . nothing . . .

CHAPTER 40

Epitaph

Someday – Slain Jane (From the multiplatinum, Grammy-winning album *Bitch Perfect*)

Don't you dare piss me off, baby,
You couldn't cope if you drove me crazy.
So just love me how I am,
Accept me how I am.
Believe I am what I tell you,
'Cos what you don't know,
Can't hurt you.
(And there's a whole lot of me that could.)
And who the hell knows?
If you keep treating me good,
Kissing my toes,
And telling me my ass hole smells like a rose,
Someday I may even love you too.

CHAPTER 41

The Urban Legend Investigation People

Warrior quickly crossed the room and retrieved his hunting knife from Jane's forehead. He had to tug hard to pull it free—the ten-inch blade had gone all the way through her head.

After getting the knife out, he stepped back from the dead woman and regarded her corpse.

"Yeah, she really was allergic to mirrors," Ninja said, stepping up beside Warrior. "But, man, you didn't have to friggin' kill her, did ya?"

"Yeah I did. She was planning on killing us."

"Shit. Dude, I was planning on interviewing her."

Warrior smirked. "Ask Ghost to interview her. I suspect they're busy getting reacquainted at this very moment."

Playboy was in the meantime bent over Miss Media. "It's okay, she's still breathing. But fuck, dudes, did you see the way Jane redirected those taser wires towards her? It was like a movie, man. Like a real ninja in action." He smirked at his cousin. "Not an overweight pretend fighter like your fat ass."

"My Kung Fu is in my mind," Ninja retorted. "It is great and mighty when things are megabytey."

Speaking in a sober voice, Warrior said, "Man down. She killed Avatar."

Playboy and Ninja gaped at him. "Huh? Ain't he just unconscious too?" Ninja asked.

Warrior shook his head. "No, our girl was playing for keeps." He pointed down at Avatar's crumpled body. Two bright streams of blood had run from the thin man's nose and stained his blue shirt purple. "I recognized that strike she used on him," Warrior explained. "It's from some ancient martial art called hono. That shit's as dangerous as snakebite. That's why I used the knife on her. If I'd let her be, she could've had us all dead in minutes."

Ninja's face had turned white. "This is the second TULIP casualty on this mission."

Warrior nodded back. "And both of those the guys who told us to leave this lady alone." He looked at Jane with great respect. She was splayed untidily across the couch, with that coin-slot hole in her head from which a thick rope of blood had spilled over her face. "Yeah, this lady was something else; she deserved to be a legend. I'd have loved to have met her socially."

Playboy looked at Ninja. "So what now?"

"We stick to the plan . . . we wait for Media to wake up and then we check our recordings. We've definitely got enough footage and proof for the website."

"I mean . . ." Playboy explained, "what do we do about these frigging bodies?"

Warrior patted him on the shoulder. "Don't worry about it, buddy. I'll think of something. In Jane's case, best thing to do will be to drive her van back home tonight and leave her inside it, along with sufficient proof to let the police know she's the one responsible for all those evil surgeries they've been investigating."

Playboy nodded. "Yeah, that sounds like a decent plan."

Ninja heaved a heavy sigh, then said, "Guys, we've a bigger problem than we envisaged."

"Huh? What are you talking about?" Playboy asked.

The obese man looked upset. "Unfortunately, we can't use any of the footage we've recorded tonight on our website." He pointed to the dead woman. "I for one don't want to get tied up in a murder rap."

"The recordings will clearly show it was self-defense."

Ninja shook his head. "Vigilantism will still get us all sent to jail forever."

Playboy looked stumped. "Damn. All this work, two of our best friends dead, and no one'll ever know what happened?"

Ninja nodded. "Except we anonymously upload the film we make to a ghost server somewhere and let everyone download it from there. But, then no one'll know who cracked the legend. I'll even need to blur out our faces in the video."

Warrior laughed. "Ha ha ha! I'll leave you brainy guys to figure that one out. Personally I'm curious 'bout something else." He gestured around at the mirrors. "I would love to know what our girl saw in all these mirrors that made her freak out like that."

"Hey, guys," Ninja suddenly said in a very worried voice, "I think you'd better take a look at this."

"What?"

***

They'd forgotten about Jane. Now though, as the three members of TULIP stared at the dead redhead on the couch, they were horrified to see that her body was splitting open.

It was weird to see a woman's body opening up like a clam shell, the split beginning from the hole in her head made by Warrior's knife, and extending down through her face and neck and into her body as though God were performing a divine autopsy on her. The bloody split ripped through Jane and her clothes all the way down to her anus.

It was even weirder to see what was *inside* Jane: A creature in a black suit. A man-shape with a giant rabbit head on its shoulders. A rabbit-headed man with lion-like teeth and reptilian hands that ended in long black claws. Huge evil-looking claws that shoved aside the halves of Insane Jane's corpse as it hauled its gore-streaked body out. It was draped in torn intestines and detached kidneys and fragments of liver and whatnot.

Behind and beyond Jane's torn viscera, her inner body seemed filled by a well of blackness from which the demonic form was emerging.

"What the hell?" Warrior gasped and quickly backed off towards his cache of weapons.

After an uncomfortable pause when it looked around the living room and seemed to be sizing things up, the rabbit-headed creature spurted out of Jane's corpse in a rush and grabbed Ninja.

The creature towered over the fat man by at least a foot. Though its head was that of a white rabbit, it also had ram-like horns. It bared its long carnivore teeth at Ninja.

Ninja began trembling with fear. The creature's pink eyes glowed with a dire rage.

"Who-who . . . w-wh-what . . . are-are-are you?" Ninja stuttered, his gaze darting from the monster holding him down to the dead woman. Insane Jane now looked as if a bomb had exploded inside her.

Like a cracked walnut, her head lay in two separate halves. Her entire torso was a massive hole. Her innards were displaced all over the couch she'd died on.

Ninja gaped back up at the monster. "Who-who-who . . . ?"

"My name," said the demon creature, "is Mr. Floppyears. Jane was a good friend of mine."

Warrior had by now reached his bag of weapons and was pulling out a shotgun from it. Playboy had meanwhile moved across the room to get out of both Warrior's and the demon's way. This was completely unexpected.

"Wha-wha-what d-d-do you wa-wa-wa-want with us?" Ninja blubbered at Mr. Floppyears.

Mr. Floppyears laughed, giving them a terrifying impression of a giant cartoon rabbit. "Why, food of course, friends! You in particular are nice and juicy and plump."

And next thing, the demon punched a hand right into Ninja's chest and tore out his heart. He dropped Ninja, who collapsed to the floor, not quite dead yet, but rapidly expiring, with gaping disbelief on his face and a gaping and bleeding hole in his chest.

Mr. Floppyears popped Ninja's heart into his mouth and took a bite. "Human hearts are so delicious," he said, with blood dripping all over his suit. "Hearts were one thing Jane would never feed me— because their removal would kill the victim and she was hung up on never killing anyone, the silly little filly . . ." He wolfed down the rest of Ninja's heart, then grinned at Warrior and Playboy. "But seeing as I'm going to kill you two anyway for what you did to Jane, I can eat your hearts without worrying about her scruples."

"Eat this instead," Warrior said, letting off a shotgun blast at Mr. Floppyears' head.

The demon was blown backwards. He collapsed onto Jane, but immediately got up again. He looked unharmed, but very angry.

"Don't make me mad. I get even hungrier when I'm mad."

Warrior fired again, but by now Mr. Floppyears was in motion, moving faster than the eye could track. Warrior kept shooting, turning while doing so, but every shot missed its target.

"Where'd he go?" Playboy asked. "Where the fuck did he go?" Warrior's shotgun had just clicked empty and Mr. Floppyears had simultaneously vanished. Playboy now had a gun too—a pistol—and was looking around the room with a scared expression on his cover-boy face.

"Yeah, where *did* the bunny son-of-a-bitch go?" Warrior growled. He flung the shotgun aside, then dipped into his weapon bag for a machine gun and cocked it. "Hey, you goddamned murderin' rabbit, show yourself!"

"I'm up here, friends." The voice came from above them both.

As they both stared up at the impossible sight of the demon 'lying' on the ceiling, Mr. Floppyears' right hand came down and tangled in Warrior's hair.

Before Warrior could either shoot or extricate himself, Mr. Floppyears' other hand made a quick circle around Warrior's neck, with one of his black fingernails slicing deep into its skin all the way around.

Next, Mr. Floppyears gave a sharp tug, and all the skin on Warrior's head—his scalp and face, along with all the neck skin above the talon-cut—came right off his skull.

Warrior dropped his machine gun and howled with pain.

Mr. Floppyears dropped to the living room floor. Once right-side-up again, he ate Warrior's face, hair and all, in two massive gulps.

Warrior had his hands pressed to his skinless head. Both hands were red from all the blood gushing out between his fingers. "Shoot the fucker!" he yelled at Playboy. "Shoot him! Blow his fucking brains—!"

Warrior went limp as Mr. Floppyears punched a hole in his chest and tore out his heart too. The demon flung Warrior aside, then popped the dying man's heart into his mouth and began chewing on it.

Then he turned to face Playboy.

Playboy had seen enough. He'd been pissing his pants ever since the demon had ripped Warrior's entire face and scalp off, a feat he knew wasn't naturally possible. Now, after a final dismayed look at the messy hole in his faceless friend's body, he dropped his gun and ran.

He didn't head for the hallway: there were too many corpses in the way now. Instead, he headed for the French doors to the outside. Just a flick of the lock and he'd have escaped this insanity.

He was undoing the lock when he felt the demon's presence behind him. It wasn't sound that alerted him to the fact that he'd been caught. No, this thing that called itself 'Mr. Floppyears' exuded a psychic reek of pure evil. Playboy felt the terror of its presence behind him like a drenching of icy sewage.

"NOOOOOO!" he screamed as he felt the demon's hot scaly hands wrapping around his neck and pulling him backwards into the living room. "NOOOOO!"

But there was no mercy or salvation. Mr. Floppyears' hand was already penetrating his back and shattering his rib cage. And then Playboy felt the excruciating agony of his heart being ripped out of him. He had a moment of lucid incredulity when he felt incredibly 'empty' inside, then he was tossed down to the living room floor, where he was treated, in the moments before his inevitable death, to the spectacle of watching a demon feast on his heart.

"Delicious," Mr. Floppyears was saying as he chewed on Playboy's heart. "Just delicious." He pointed a bloody finger over at his dead protégé. "Oh, I'm most certain even Jane would approve."

CHAPTER 42

Miss Media

She revived to a burning smell, like smelling salts so pungent they'd caught on fire.

She was woozy. She recalled what had happened:

I tazed myself in the boobs. Damn that woman!

That was about as far as her recollections went. She struggled to wake up fully, but her brain was like a ball bouncing in and out of consciousness.

At some point during this, she became aware that she wasn't on the floor any more. She was being carried, borne off somewhere, hopefully away from the fire. Along with this rescue came an intense stink of roast meat.

It smells delicious, she thought.

She'd have loved to be worried about the fire, but she couldn't gather enough of her senses together to really bother about what was happening to her.

Maybe later. At the moment it smells like the guys are celebrating Jane's capture with a barbeque.

She faded out again.

When next she bounced back into awareness of her surroundings, she was no longer being carried. Now she was seated upright in the front passenger seat of a vehicle in motion—it seemed to be a van. She was strapped in with the seatbelt.

She looked outside. It was still night, the sky as black as the heart of death.

She looked left, at the driver. The driver was a man with a rabbit's head. He was eating something that looked like raw intestines.

Oh, I'm still dreaming, she thought calmly. *That was quite a bump to the head I took back there.*

The rabbit-man noticed that she was awake. He stopped eating the raw intestines for a moment. He reached over and patted her head with a bloody lizard-foot-like hand.

"Relax, little girl," he said in a soothing voice, "I'm your new friend, Mr. Floppyears. There was a huge fire but you're safe now. I'm taking you back home."

She nodded. He popped the raw intestines back into his mouth and concentrated on the road.

Yeah, the vagina fuck I am frigging dreaming, she thought.

After a while, she fell asleep again.

EPILOGUE: THE HUNGER LOOP

Three dawns ago, on Sunday morning, Miss Media had woken up inside a parked black van. The truly weird thing about this, however, was that though she'd earlier dreamt—*I was dreaming for sure*—that she'd been a passenger in the van, she'd woken up in the driver's seat, belted in and with her foot on the brake pedal and her hand on the gearshift.

That had been oddity number one.

Oddity number two was that she'd apparently driven herself (though she preferred to think she'd been driven) over to Insane Jane's house. The black van had been parked inside Jane's garage, and, on getting out of the vehicle, she'd discovered she had a complete set of the house keys in her pocket.

The next oddity was how easily she'd settled into Jane's house, as if it were her own. The house felt eerily natural to her, as if, though coming here for the first time, she was in reality a rabbit returning to its warm and safe burrow.

It was odd too how she now instinctively knew a lot of things that she'd previously had no knowledge of. And also how her attitude to several acts that she'd previously considered both inhumane and obscene had undergone a radical change literally overnight.

One of the pivotal incidences on her arriving 'home' (as she thought of the place now), was her first trip downstairs to the basement.

The basement had both a concealed hallway entrance and a security code for this hidden door. She'd found the entrance without the slightest difficulty. Entering the passcode was even easier; the correct number sequence had come to her mind as vividly as if she was viewing it on paper.

The door had clicked open. She'd descended the stairs and stepped inside Insane Jane's basement. She'd stood there gaping in awe and delight.

The place was perfect. The dissecting table with its array of scalpels. The freezers with their array of meats. The books. The tools. The grinder. The portable incinerator that Jane was building to get rid of 'evidence' scraps . . .

She'd looked it all over and grinned. *I just need to fetch the two suitcases of surgical equipment from the rear of the van. And that icebox filled with meat . . .*

Back upstairs, she'd flicked through several of the medical texts in the living room bookshelves. These too she understood clearly, now discovering a previously buried interest in human surgery.

There were no mirrors in the house, but that was just fine by her. She had a deep impression—the knowledge resided in her now—that she didn't want to look into any mirrors ever again: she'd hate what they'd show her.

All of Jane's banking information and passwords, every single piece of knowledge the dead woman had ever possessed, was right now at Miss Media's own fingertips. She could even perfectly sign Jane's signature. She didn't know how this was possible, but she liked it. It made her feel powerful, made her feel somehow divine.

And speaking of fingertips, Miss Media had already discovered that she no longer had any fingerprints. Very strange, but she liked that too. A lack of fingerprints would make fulfilling her newly discovered purpose in life all the easier.

Most important of all, she now felt hungry. This was a deep ravaging hunger for sweet and tender human flesh. Not whole bodies. No, not at all. She just desired the choicest bits, which of course, would vary from person to person. All she needed was just that perfect part of each of them. And she wouldn't either hurt or kill them while taking that part of them that was rightfully hers.

She was a cannibal goddess and they were mere mortals and her prey.

***

After returning from work in Boston on Monday, Miss Media had driven out to Playboy's cottage to check out the situation there.

There was nothing left there—the fire had gutted everything, including the TULIP surveillance van they'd parked outside the house.

It was an incredibly destructive and (to the police) completely inexplicable case of arson.

On a positive note, she'd gathered that there were no bodies found inside the gutted remains of the house. That was fine then. No bodies of course meant no crime.

She'd smiled: *Just another urban mystery for TULIP to investigate.*

***

At about 7 p.m. that Wednesday evening, her front doorbell rang. She hurried out to see who it was.

She was pleasantly surprised. "Scott? Scott Hamilton?"

"Jane Summers?"

Wow, now this is interesting, Miss Media thought. She'd known Insane Jane was dating a 'Scott,' but she'd had no idea that it was this one, her ex from three years back. They'd broken up mainly because she couldn't stand his clingy daughter Caitlin.

Scott was clearly as surprised to see her as she was to see him: "Jane, what are *you* doing here?"

She smiled. "Scotty, I should ask *you* that."

He looked confused, then worried. "This is my girlfriend's house. Is she back home now? I've been calling her for three days now. I've been here four times already and also to her place of work, and I already filed a Missing Persons report."

"I'm sorry, Scotty, but I'm confused too," Miss Media lied. "See, Jane called me on the phone on Saturday afternoon—we've been friends since high school—and said that she had to leave town for an unspecified destination and might not be returning soon. She said she was in huge trouble but couldn't explain."

"She said that?"

Miss Media nodded. She gestured back inside. "She asked me to housesit for her, that's why I'm here." Then, putting her coldly calculating superb mind to work (she'd always known she was super-smart, but had had no idea she was so amoral too), she smiled at the bewildered man. "But, please forgive me. I must have lost my manners, leaving you standing outside here. Please come on in."

As Scott Hamilton pondered her words and stepped inside her lair, Insane Jane smiled at his backside. *No meat there or anywhere else on him for that matter. He's too skinny and too old to taste any good.*

But then she remembered Scott had a wonderful-looking penis.

But, my basement is packed full of meat, and if it's penis meat I want, I've currently got four manhoods on ice from the guys in TULIP—Ninja's looks particularly delicious. Still, I'll hold Scotty in reserve. There's really no point in eating Scotty's dick anyway—the sex was always good.

And besides, the way she viewed it, Scott Hamilton still owed her a wedding ring.

She grinned evilly. *And if Caitlin makes a nuisance of herself this time—there's always the basement.*

Miss Media/Insane Jane locked the front door and hurried after Scott.

She remembered her pet name for Scott back then and a bittersweet smile creased her lips. 'Honeybunch,' that's what she'd always called him.

But then he'd begun using the term for his daughter too. *That* had been the last straw that ended their relationship.

But not this time. Now she grinned. "Hey, honeybunch, can I get you something to drink?"

And so the cycle began again.

The End

ABOUT THE AUTHOR

Wol-vriey is Nigerian, and quite tall.

He believes there actually are things that go bump in the night.

He writes horror fiction—for adults only, please. And also some surrealist stuff.

Wol-vriey blogs at: *http://oddityfarm.wordpress.com*

WOL-VRIEY

BIZARRO AND TRANSGRESSIVE FICTION

BOSTON POSH (BUD MALONE #1)

In 2028 AD, the USA is a nation ravaged by hungry dragons and dinosaurs. In Boston, Massachusetts, private eye Bud Malone is hired to rescue a kidnapped heiress. But nothing is as it seems.

Malone works to unravel a tangled web involving Boston Chinatown, a 200-year-old woman with a 9-year-old body, white robots, a human-liver-eating psychopath, a golem, a porcelain dragon, and a snake goddess with a crush on him. There's also a woman obsessed with chicken sex. Then Malone meets Posh Lane, a gorgeous call girl who's desperate to quit her pimp.

Romantic sparks ignite between Posh and Malone, but Posh's past suddenly catches up with her in a BIG way. To save Posh, Malone agrees to run a quest for Earth's new rulers, the Forks. But, Malone has no idea that agreeing to the Fork's odd request will send him on the weirdest trip he's ever been on in his life.

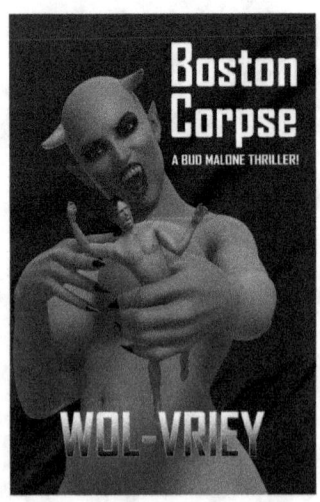

BOSTON CORPSE (BUD MALONE #2)

MAGIC CAN BE MURDER! - Drag queen Lucy Tang is back in Boston, and is hell-bent on settling her vindetta against casino owner Sookie Ling. And suddenly, Bud Malone, PI, has the case of his life to resolve.

When Boston's robot police force are baffled by a mind transfer case, they come to Malone for help. The one person who can likely help Malone out here is the witch Soledad Bathory. But Soledad seems to know a lot more than she's telling him. It's a case not made easier when Malone meets Soledad's beautiful cousin, Josephine 'Slave' Bailey. Slave has her own plans for Malone, most of which involve teaching him BDSM and making him her new Master.

Oh, and Rick Rogers owes Sookie Ling a whole lot of money, a gambling debt that's going to be literally Hell to pay!

BOSTON CORPSE - Not your average detective novel!

Burning Bulb
PUBLISHING

WOL-VRIEY
BIZARRO AND TRANSGRESSIVE FICTION

BOSTON LUST (BUD MALONE #3)

"Bless it, Father, for she has sinned."

Seven murdered gay women, all their bodies completely drained of blood. All also with large parts of their bodies dissolved away like acid has been pumped into their veins.

Bud Malone has to find the female vampire preying on Boston's lesbian population.

Then Malone meets the beautiful Trudi Carmen and the case gets even more tangled. Trudi needs Malone's help in recovering a ring that's gone missing. But how in the world is one little black ring related to either the dead women or their killer?

Resolving this case will lead Malone deep into Lucy Tang's legacy—The Abstracta. And then to the city of Genesis.

Boston Lust—Just when you thought Bean Town was safe to visit again.

HELL DANCER

Six people find themselves trapped in Detention, a nightmare realm where the demonic Schoolmaster is hell-bent on reforming them . . . until they die.

Porn superstar Venus Deluxe came to Springfield, MA to party, and next found her life hanging by a thread. One wrong answer will mean her death.

Suspended BPD detective Tanya Rockford was trying to stop one kind of violence, but found a terrifying another. With her and her companion's lives hanging in the balance, it's going to take all of her courage and resourcefulness to escape this hell she's stumbled into.

Porn stud Chad Cannon has made a career from his ten-inch penis. Here in Detention, however, it's his brains that matter. He'll soon be hoping all the pot he's smoked over the years hasn't completely messed up his memory.

The three students, Sherri, Jordan, and Mike? They were all just in the wrong place at the right time. Will anyone survive Detention? The evil Schoolmaster doesn't plan on letting that happen . . .

Burning Bulb
PUBLISHING

WOL-VRIEY
BIZARRO AND TRANSGRESSIVE FICTION

VAGINA MUNDI

Rachel Risk is a professional thief with super-strong hair that can stretch like tentacles to manipulate objects. Ashley Status has both a digitally augmented brain, and 'muscle-purses' in her arms and legs in which she stores inflatable objects—cars, guns, rocket launchers, etc.

When Raye is framed as the fall girl in a jewel robbery, the pair flee Chicago's vengeful robot gangsters and take refuge in the Hotel Bizarre, where the gorgeous 'vagina singer,' Femina, is performing for a week.

But the Hotel Bizarre is even stranger than its name suggests, and very soon Raye and Ash are involved in an deadly adventure, a struggle for survival the likes of which they'd never imagined possible—with loads of deviant sex, drugs, music, and violence at every turn. And just what is the old woman in the skin desert really doing with all those cats glued to her walls?

VAGINA MUNDI—a Bizarro Hymn in praise of WOMAN!

VEGAN VAMPIRE VAGINAS

The biggest bank heist in US history. And Tom Palmer can't remember pulling it off. And no, this isn't your standard case of amnesia. After a one-night-stand gone horribly wrong, Boston salesman Tom Palmer wakes up with a vagina implanted in his left hand. Then his day gets worse.

Tom is transported across space-time to a nightmare version of Boston, one where the Bizarro virus has transformed half the population into cannibals. Worst of all, Tom discovers that in this new Boston, he's the infamous gangster Pussypalm, wanted for robbing the Federal Reserve Bank of Boston a year ago. He also learns that the vagina in his hand is prophetic, i.e. it talks . . . after sex.

With 130 people left dead during his bank heist and six billion dollars missing, Tom knows he's living on borrowed time. It is in his best interests not to remember anything. Because once he does . . .

Burning Bulb
PUBLISHING

WOL-VRIEY
BIZARRO AND TRANSGRESSIVE FICTION

VEGAN ZOMBIE APOCALYPSE

In the post-apocalypse worlderness, zombies rule the earth. They're allergic to meat, and brains literally make them explode. Zombies now eat blood potatoes, parasitic tubers grown in the flesh of humancows corralled in maximum security farms. Two fugitives meet in the ancient ruins of Texas. The first is Soil 15-f, a womancow who's escaped her farm a week before she's due to be killed and her blood potato crop harvested. The second fugitive is Able Kane, former head necros food technician, now sentenced to death for heresy. But Soil is no ordinary humancow.

Unknown to herself, she's the vegan zombie agricultural revolution, and the zombies desperately want her back. And the necros equally desperately want Able Kane dead. He's fled with a forbidden discovery which will reshape the world for the worse if used. And Able is just hardheaded/misguided enough to use it.

MELANIE NEMESIS CATCHPOLE

In Springfield, Massachusetts, Melanie Catchpole is hired to fetch back a magic teddy bear worth millions of dollars from a warehouse across town. Problem is, the warehouse is down in Springfield's O-Zone—that totally weird sector of the city where Bizarro fell to Earth. The 'O' is a fairytale land, a place where dreams and nightmares literally live and breathe..

Worse still, the gingers—mutant cannibals—prowl the O. The gingers have already eaten everyone else Melanie's employers sent to get back the magic teddy bear.

Accompanied by the handsome but ruthless Doug Fisher (who she finds sexy but doesn't dare entrust her heart to), Melanie enters the O-Zone. Melanie and Doug are instantly caught up in an adventure they'd never have believed credible even if written as fiction . . . and Melanie's used to experiencing the very weird as the norm.

And now, additionally, there's a mystery to unravel: What does the dark, freezing-cold being called The Fixer want with Mary, the barkeep's daughter?

Burning Bulb
PUBLISHING

WOL-VRIEY
BIZARRO AND TRANSGRESSIVE FICTION

BIG TROUBLE IN LITTLE ASS

From Bizarro master storyteller Wol-vriey comes a truly weird western tale that will leave you awe-struck and on the edge of your seat...

In the town named Little Ass, tight-assed prostitute Rosa overhears a gunslinger's plans to assassinate rancher Edison Bennett. Once the badass Bennett learns of the plot, he ensures there'll be hell to pay for any attempt on his life!

Yes, it's going to take all of gunslinger Jude's shooting prowess, his eclectic collection of strange firearms, a trusty horse that requires an owners' manual, and the help of the lovely and invigorating Nell (who's EXTREMELY odd when the going gets weird), to survive the Bizarro hell that Edison Bennett unleashes in order to hold onto the land that he'd stolen from Madam Zizi.

BIZARRO 101 (A BASIC PRIMER)

Welcome to the strange place:

A collection of 37 flash fiction stories designed to introduce one to the Bizarro/New Weird Genre.

Weird, dreamy, nightmarish, absurd, sad, surreal, humorous . . . this collection of tales is all this and more.

***

"This primer is the very essence of any and all styles and types of Bizarro writing. Wol-vriey collects, distills, and bottles up these 37 tiny stories for your sensory enjoyment. This is an absolute must-read for anyone new to the genre, because it demonstrates the scope of what Bizarro is, and what it can be."
—Teresa Pollack, Bizarro commentator and blogger

Burning Bulb
PUBLISHING

WOL-VRIEY
BIZARRO AND TRANSGRESSIVE FICTION

Dr. Orgasm

Courtney Taylor is young, intelligent, beautiful, and successful. She also has a boyfriend who loves her deeply. The problem is, no matter what Courtney does, she can't climax during sex.

When Florence Rigid's communist forces destroy the city of Metaphor, Courtney and her friends Teresa, Highball, Miki, and Heather are cast into the midst of a quest to find the only person able to save the land of Innuendo—Dr. Carol Orgasm, wanted by the communists for developing the O-Pill, a wonder drug that grants women sexual ecstasy on demand.

The communists will do anything to get their hands on the O-Pill and prevent its reaching the millions of Innuendo's women. But Courtney desperately wants that pill too. And so it's now a race between Courtney and the communists to find Dr. Orgasm first.

And Courtney has no choice but to win this race. She must win it: For her own orgasm . . . and for the freedom of female sexuality everywhere.

PUSSY TRANSMISSION

Pussy Transmission were the most decadent Pop Art ensemble of the 90's. Led by the beautiful painter Isis Lynch, the trio revolutionized the art world. Then suddenly, without explanation, Pussy Transmission vanished into historical obscurity. Now, twenty years later, three women come to Lynch Place. Lily and Nina are journalists desperate to interview Isis Lynch. Raven, on the other hand, wants to find her boyfriend, who's gone missing inside Isis's house. Raven's worried—she's heard that Pussy Transmission broke up because Isis began dabbling in black magic . . . with devastating results. All three women will shortly wish they'd never left home. Particularly once the rats in Lynch Place start warning them that they're going to die . . . and Raven meets Betty Butcher, the bouncy supernatural psycho who's intent on chopping her into bits. Pussy Transmission, Baby! Just because . . .

Burning Bulb
PUBLISHING

WOL-VRIEY
BIZARRO AND TRANSGRESSIVE FICTION

GIRLS ARE NOT SMILING

Welcome To The Road Trip From Hell

Pagan is demon-possessed.

Lori is suicidal.

Britt is just terminally pissed off.

Meet three young Boston women on the run from the law, each with problems that will fuse into more than the sum of their individual parts, becoming a holocaust of sex and violence and terror, a literal rain of blood and horror and gore and evil.

And if that wasn't already bad enough, Pagan's pet demon is slowly transforming her into something both unspeakable and unholy. Truly, these girls aren't smiling.

BLUE NIGHTMARES

Consummate EVIL is coming.   It is relentless and unavoidable. It is Blue.

Jessica Schreiber is seeing things. Very horrible things. Since arriving in Raynham for what should have been a relaxing vacation, she's been seeing *The Big Blue*.

Jessica is smelling things too—dead and rotting things that she can't see. She is sure those dead and rotting things are dead people. Lots of dead people.

Jessica's worst nightmares will soon become her reality. Her reality will soon become a terrifying nightmare.

The tentacled residents of the House of Death have a lot that they wish to show Jessica Schreiber. They have a lot that they wish to tell her. But will she survive long enough to learn their lessons?

Burning Bulb
PUBLISHING

WOL-VRIEY
BIZARRO AND TRANSGRESSIVE FICTION

BRAINCHEW

It was supposed to be a simple jewel heist, but it went badly wrong. Chuck got shot and died.

Lance hid his friend's corpse in the Pleasant Street Cemetery. But that was a big mistake—there was something undead, something extremely hungry . . . something eXXXtremely horrible, buried in the Pleasant Street Cemetery.

And Lance had just woken it up.

They called the monster Brainchew because it ate brains. Human brains. And it preferred those brains fresh from the heads . . . of the living.

And now it was awake again, Brainchew planned on feeding big-time tonight. Oh hell yes, it did.

BRAINCHEW 2: OUT OF THEIR HEADS

After Tiff Hooper recognizes Josh Penham, the man who abducted her and kept her in his basement and abused her, she brings her three friends to Raynham for a night of well-deserved revenge on him.

Only things don't go according to plan.

It is never a good idea to leave a corpse in Raynham's Pleasant Street Cemetery. You run the very real risk of awakening what lies underground there. And that thing—Brainchew—is more horrible and more evil than anything the average mind conceives of even in its worst nightmares.

Brainchew is back! And this time the monster is extra-hungry. But there are plenty of delicious human brains about tonight, and Brainchew intends to eat them all before dawn.

Burning Bulb
PUBLISHING

WOL-VRIEY
BIZARRO AND TRANSGRESSIVE FICTION

DARIA: AN EROTIC NIGHTMARE

Even the best laid women can go wrong.

Daria Simpson is HUNGRY. She's HUNGRY for sex and bloodshed and death.

Shelly Parker just wanted to have a threesome with her boyfriend Craig and her best friend Erica. Everything was shaping up nicely for their weekend of sexual fun and games, until they stopped at the creepy Crossway Diner and met Daria.

From the moment they met Daria, EVERYTHING went wrong for them; and it went wrong in the most horrific and terrifying of ways!

Daria: Paranormal service has been resumed.

WET BONES

Greg is about learning the hard way that you don't mess with Aunt Grace.

Nine completely fleshless skeletons recovered in the Massachusetts woods. Two detectives on the trail of a horrible, hungry monster.

Broken-hearted Allie Jackson has a date with a creature from Hell.

Things are about to get well out of hand for everyone, and in horrifying, terrifying ways they don't expect.

Burning Bulb
PUBLISHING

WOL-VRIEY
BIZARRO AND TRANSGRESSIVE FICTION

MR. UGLY

When a rotting corpse appears and starts butchering Raynham's youths, there's really only one question that needs answering:

Is this faceless and rotting monster Peter Howard, or isn't it?

Problem is, Peter Howard died 15 years ago. So how can he possibly be back from the dead and murdering people with such relentless and incredible brutality?

Peter's mother Malicia, who's just been released from the lunatic asylum may have the answers to the crazy puzzle, but the two detectives investigating the deaths don't even know the right questions to ask her yet.

BRUTAL

Jane Winters is 28 years old.

She works as a checkout cashier in a department store. She's an attractive woman with a winning personality. She has both a photographic memory and an I.Q. of 189.

She's met the man of her dreams.

But she's also a cannibal with a unique and very scary mode of operation.

The group known as TULIP (The Urban Legend Investigation People) are out to either prove or disprove the legend of Insane Jane.

But have TULIP bitten off more than they can chew?

Burning Bulb
PUBLISHING